"Adria Libolt tells compassionate, tough stories about young people in reform schools and adults in maximum-security prisons. "She layers each story with nuance, irony, and breadth to show why she feels it is a thin line between a prisoner and the rest of us. Even as she acknowledges the dangers, she feels safer in prison than outside. "This book will complicate your perspective on prisoners and the prison system."

—Linda R. Peckham
Author of *The Pocket Hotline for Writers*

"Adria Libolt offers an insightful, compelling perspective on the myriad of issues surrounding our country's corrections systems. This 'inside' look at prison life would be extremely valuable to anyone in a position like mine that requires us to not only take a critical, thoughtful look at what's happening in our corrections system, but to make policy decisions that will have far-reaching consequences for the state and for the employees and prisoners closest to those systems."

—Joan Bauer
Legislator
Michigan House of Representatives

A Deputy Warden's Reflections
on Prison Work

A Deputy Warden's Reflections on Prison Work

Adria L. Libolt

RESOURCE *Publications* · Eugene, Oregon

A DEPUTY WARDEN'S REFLECTIONS ON PRISON WORK

Resource Publications
An Imprint of Wipf and Stock Publishers
199 W. 8th Ave., Suite 3
Eugene, OR 97401
www.wipfandstock.com

ISBN 13: 978-1-61097-872-9

Manufactured in the U.S.A.

To Clay

Contents

Foreword

YOU WOULD PROBABLY DO a double take seeing Adria Libolt behind the warden's desk or anyplace else inside a prison, even a prison housing women. She is petite, soft-spoken, and very "proper." A former researcher who decided to become part of the action, in this book she relates her experiences and observations of prison life, each experience a short story in itself. Each one relates a lesson, expresses a value, or warns about judgments that Libolt herself had to learn.

As a coworker in the corrections field, I found Libolt to be straightforward, honest, considerate, and respectful of others whether they were superior or subordinate in rank, a coworker or another agency representative, an offender or offender family member. While some, and maybe many, thought it peculiar that a woman of her makeup would be working in the prison setting, she quickly gained their confidence and provided the leadership her various positions demanded. As an experienced corrections administrator, I am impressed with the details she points out in her writings, details many corrections workers might overlook or consider too trivial to be concerned with. This is especially true in regard to actions dealing with other humans.

This I learned long before I read her book when presenting speeches as the corrections director. I would often break the ice by telling the fictitious story of attending a banquet at one of the prisons. Baked potatoes were served and I asked the inmate server if I could have an extra pat of butter for my potato. "No sir" he responded. "One potato, one pat of butter." I thought to myself, "This guy doesn't realize who I am." I beckoned for him to come back and inquired, "Do you know who I am?" "No sir" he replied. "Well, I'm the Director of the Department of Corrections. I'm in charge of all the Wardens, I'm in charge of the Parole Board, I'm in charge of Probation and Parole officers and correction centers." He said, "I see sir. And do you know who I am?" I had a reputation for knowing the names of inmates, but did not know this one. Sheepishly, I said, "No sir, I don't. Who are you?" Without hesitation, he loudly proclaimed, *"I'm the guy in charge of the butter!"*

While I assume most folks saw the humor in the story, Adria recognized that everyone needs to feel in charge of something they can be proud of and that we need to acknowledge and respect that. She also pointed out that others might not ascribe the same importance to our positions as we do.

Throughout the book, Libolt relates stories of people—and not just prisoners—not willing to accept responsibilities for their actions, many times trying to make others appear responsible for their misconduct or poor judgment. One story reminded me of an interview with a prisoner serving a life sentence for killing and robbing a Detroit taxi driver. He was debasing murderers as if he wasn't one too. When I brought this to his attention, he denied being a murderer. "I didn't kill that cab driver" he proclaimed. "He committed suicide." "How do you figure that?" I asked. His outrageous response: "I was in the back seat and made it clear to him that if he turned around, I would shoot him. He turned around. He committed suicide." The prisoner had repeated this rationale enough that he had convinced himself that he was not responsible for the killing.

If you have worked with troubled people, you will be reminded of encounters you have experienced. If your work has taken you in other directions, you will appreciate the exposure.

Robert Brown, Jr., Corrections Consultant and former Director of the Michigan Department of Corrections

Preface and Acknowledgments

I HAVE BEEN ENJOYING the freedom of writing this book in my head for some time. I was writing it when I walked through prison housing areas during a quiet time, like when count was being taken. There, I often saw prisoners who seemed to be deep in thought, and I wondered whether landing in a cell and being suddenly thrown upon your thoughts was difficult for a prisoner who had been active in the community. Perhaps it was a gift like the advice given to brothers by the Desert Fathers of the fourth and fifth century who, when asked for a word, said, "Go sit in your cell, and your cell will teach you everything."

For some freedom may come from being confined in a cell or a 4x4 cubicle. For me a certain 4x4 cubicle was a problem, but solitary experiences of writing, thinking, or dreaming about my years working in prisons not so much. I never felt as though I "locked myself up" in order to put words on the page. I was never isolated. In fact, through my writing doors opened up for me and unlocked some of the ambivalence I had experienced working in prisons.

Yet writing this book entailed a giving up of sorts. Sometimes I gave up socializing to write. I didn't always allow myself to be distracted by a sunny day, or jogging and walking, a room in need of dusting, or a call from someone.

Writing this entailed another kind of giving up too, a giving up of myself. For once I began giving others my writing to read, they knew something about my heart.

Writing entailed conversation with others. It meant going out the door to a community to dialogue with others who read and write. Althea Gibson, the famous tennis player, reminds us that, "No matter what accomplishments you achieve, somebody helps you."

I thank the people who helped me by reading the words, each page and chapter. I soon trusted them to tell me if what I was saying made sense, was clear, and was authentic. Their reactions and careful critique were important, and helped me to convey both what was necessary and what improved the writing. Sometimes they affirmed what I wrote. Other times, they sent me back to the desk with suggestions because, as one friend says, "that dog doesn't hunt."

I am indebted to many people in this community for their help with this book. Linda Peckham, a fellow instructor at Lansing Community College and mentor to many writing students, taught me I had stories worth telling and introduced me to a community of writers. Among those writers was Phil Kline whose encouragement and optimism kept me coming to writing meetings on the coldest winter evenings. Dr. Carol Scot's sharp eye kept me from veering off course by reminding me about organization, changing topics too quickly, and whiplash. Dee Cassidy, a master of punctuation and grammar, suggested commas and periods and filled in empty spaces in more ways than one. Nancy Kelly and Alan Harris, who came later, gave me ideas and insights with good humor.

My writing friend, the late Betty Drobac, introduced me to the Michigan State University Community Club of Creative Writers, and I found there a group of spirited readers and writers whose keen literary criticism and writing delighted me. They are Karen Benson, Judy Birn, Kathy Esselman, Lyn Farquhar, Jean McManus, Laina Melvin, Kate O'Neill, Sally Pratt, and Clarice Thompson.

Dr. Lois Bader, a passionate professor and advocate for literacy and the executive director of Capital Area Literacy Coalition where I volunteered as a tutor and then worked, freely shared her knowledge, reviewed my manuscript, and was generous in so many other ways too.

An intellectual friend of mine, Harold Ellens, who has written many books and was one of the first to read my entire manuscript when it was completed, was attentive, taking an active interest in having me pursue the publication of this book.

I have learned much from Ulrike Guthrie who is a responsive, patient, and astute editor and who also greatly encouraged me and made recommendations that improved my writing.

Christian Amondson at Wipf and Stock was exceptionally helpful and thoroughly and promptly addressed each question I had. The materials provided and his responses kept me informed at each step of the publishing process.

I am especially grateful to many leaders in Corrections who assured me I wasn't going crazy on days when I vacillated between, "Hallelujah, it's better than I expected!" and, like Dorothy Parker, asked, "What fresh new hell is this?"

I worked in Corrections with some good leaders. When I began in the Program Bureau Perry Johnson was the impressive and good Director of the Michigan Department of Corrections. Deputy Director Bob Brown, who later became the Director of the Michigan Department of Corrections, was on the other side of my cubicle wall. He says I was "soft-spoken." I didn't want to disturb him, but I never heard him raise his voice either. Perhaps he roared sometimes, but he was always kind and sensible with a sense of humor. I learned early on that even with all his responsibilities he knew the importance of knowing more about the prisoners than the crimes they committed. He enjoyed interacting with them.

I am grateful to Denise Quarles who was the Regional Administrator of seventeen prisons but always had time to answer my many questions, and who had the unique ability to ask me the very questions I had not thought to ask. She was an answer to prayer at several critical times in my career.

I admire Sherry Burt, another thoughtful friend who is always respectful and whose knowledge of policy and procedures and loyalty I value greatly.

John Makowski was a leader and warden whose progressive and creative methods brought forth the best work in employees and who had an uncanny ability to persuade employees to work hard while enjoying themselves.

Tekla Miller early on encouraged me to write and was an example of a warden with tremendous esprit de corps both in a women's and a men's prison. Carol Howes, another good leader and warden of Florence Crane Correctional Facility where I had the opportunity to work with women prisoners, offered them programs with possibilities for their future.

To many officers, case managers, and other supervisors who worked to make Corrections a better place, I am grateful.

I am thankful that Rev. Rich Rienstra, a pastor of restorative justice, reached out to me and many prison volunteers and became the first pastor of Celebration Fellowship, a congregation of prisoners meeting within a prison. My life has been enriched seeing prisoners whose lives are being transformed. I have met returning citizens who have taught me much about the burdens and stigma of having prison records and about their resilience. I am amazed at what my friend and colleague Monica does to make their lives better.

In my church community, many came together to help ex-offenders. Among them are Erv and Barb Mosher, Bob Leonard, Ralph Monsma, Ron Bosma, Teresa Ritsema, Alfred and Richard Laurence, Judy Hamilton, Jan Mason, and O'Neal Carter and, from other church denominations, Bob and Pat Heriford, Frank Dennis, Len Hill, Liz Chaney, and Victor Asbury. Thanks to Derrick F. Jones, Executive Director of the Michigan Prisoner Reentry Initiative, and Matthew Walker, parole agent of Ingham County Parole of the Michigan Department of Corrections, who attended our meetings and gave us crucial information.

I thank my Mother who instilled in me a love of reading and learning at an early age.

Finally, I am most of all grateful for my husband Clay, the love of my life, whose support of me throughout my Corrections career was a source of strength, and whose scholarship and writing on justice in the church continue to inspire me.

Introduction

PEOPLE ARE SURPRISED WHEN I tell them that I worked for years in prisons. They associate prisons with stabbings, riots, rapes, and other dangers. I am a small physically unprepossessing woman—not their image of a prison deputy warden. I am often asked if I worked directly with prisoners. I did. Along the way I learned that life in a prison is not what most people expected. It's this inside perspective that I present in this book.

I did not set out thinking I'd work in prisons. My education prepared me to be a teacher or administrator. While I worked on my graduate degree in education at the University of Michigan, I began evaluating a program in the state facilities for juvenile delinquents, facilities often referred to as reform schools. Many of the names of these youth were familiar to me later when I began my work in the Michigan Department of Corrections (MDOC). I realized that criminal behavior is often entrenched; juvenile delinquents frequently become adult prisoners.

When I began working in the Department of Corrections, I continued evaluating programs, this time in prisons. I enrolled in Michigan State University, intending to acquire another degree in educational research. Evaluation was and remains valuable experience. Program evaluation, beneficial for determining the effectiveness of programs, left an indelible impression on me, marking my life in Corrections. One outcome was that I continued to ask questions and search for answers in all the prisons where I worked.

But I wanted a change from program evaluation, and thought prison work would give me a challenge.

My first position at Huron Valley Men's Facility opened my eyes to what prisons and prisoners are really like. A few days after I began my work, I faced a hungry, persistent mob of media personnel who wanted to know how and why a serious escape had occurred. The dangerous prisoners there caused many critical incidents during the time I worked at "the Valley," and made the media a rather regular presence at the prison.

I recognized early on that the media and popular culture often focus on the dramatic and the extreme. Movies, as a reflection of the culture's desires and fears, portray prisoners as either evil or, as in *Shawshank Redemption*, charismatic and heroic. Who could not identify or sympathize with the star prisoners played by Morgan Freedman and Tim Robbins and dislike the employees who became the bad guys?

One of the themes of this book is that we are not that different than prisoners—even the most dangerous and manipulative inmates. Small indiscretions, like "finding" a state writing pen in my purse, and large ones, like taking a car which did not belong to me, convinced me that even with advantages of education and a supportive family, I was not immune to committing crimes. Employees in prisons break the law, and risk their careers because of their involvement with prisoners. We are all connected—in good and in harmful ways—and that is both one of the advantages and drawbacks of working in this environment.

Some readers will protest that they have nothing in common with those who commit horrendous crimes. I too think there are crimes I wouldn't commit. But as long as I think of prisoners as "the other," I will not have compassion for any of them. Prisoners often respond with dignity in a dehumanizing environment. I write about a mentally ill prisoner who responded correctly to an employee even though that employee didn't use the best judgment or the recommendations in policy. Many of the prisoners work to do what is right in preparation for their release. Many have been humbled and know how dependent they are on staff. They joke, laugh, and cry in a place where they need quite some grit to survive. Perhaps it's not surprising that it can be easier to relate to some prisoners than to some co-workers.

For a short time I was fortunate to work with women prisoners, a large percentage of whom have been victimized. I learned to appreciate their demands for more communication and participation in decisions affecting them, although their values about being women often seemed so different than mine. Policies that protect women prisoners from on-going victimization are a must. I hope to convey what it is like for women to be in prison where they have little privacy, are away from their children, and are justifiably apprehensive about further victimization.

I was frequently asked if I was afraid too, a question asked more often of women than men. There are reasons for fear, though most employees are not paralyzed by it, or they could not continue to work in prisons. Of course, fear is personal. There are no guarantees of safety in prisons or the community either, where there is less control than in the confines of a prison. When I thought about frightening experiences, I recalled events that occurred *outside* the prison. In fact one can become comfortable in the routines of a prison, where it seems everything is operating in good order. Prisons, with their focus on keeping the environment safe, are equipped with security staff, a myriad of devices and technology—even though all that doesn't keep bad incidents from occurring. Being alert and cautious, so essential in prisons, is important anywhere. There are desperate offenders in prison and criminals in the community rattling our nerves as we walk through dark parking lots at night.

My fears paled in comparison to the prisoners' fears. A telephone conversation with a prisoner's mother, afraid for him, and my frustration about assuring his safety, concerned me greatly. Prisoners and their families fear assaults, rape, and even death at the hands of other prisoners.

It's the variety and surprise of prison life that I try to portray in this book. As always when remembering experiences and then writing about them, I tell what was significant but also what the incident says about life in prisons.

I have included experiences selectively rather than as a sequence of events or chronological account of *"in the beginning I worked in a prison and now at the end my present work is with ex-offenders."* I am reminded of a cartoon I saw some time ago. A man comes into the room where his wife is watching TV. She, obviously responding to his question, says, "It's a love story. Nobody is ahead."

The meanings of stories are in the spaces between the lines. I largely want the reader to interpret them. I sometimes draw on past experiences and some incidents that did not occur in prison but which inform my experiences there. Others who experienced the same event would tell a different story.

Having said that, my stories are true as I recollect them, except that I have changed most names of employees and prisoners to protect their identities. I guard against faulty memories by keeping journals and reading. Factual material in the book sometimes justifies what I think or opposes it. I wanted to know if my experiences have a basis in what others report about prisons and Corrections. I wrote about my first position in

Corrections in evaluation, and although I left that work my search for answers and the need for studies and research remains a part of me.

Some of you may read this book because you are persuaded that the work in prisons or with ex-offenders is interesting and rewarding. Criminal justice professionals may want their students to read about perspectives of prison work as well as studies. Public officials may want to explore how to reduce both the financial and social costs of incarceration, and what it is like to assist prisoners coming to the community looking for work and housing. Perhaps others, personally hurt by crime, will give prisoners and ex-offenders some chances they need. To those of you already working or incarcerated in prisons, strive for justice tempered with mercy even when you are in complex situations where there do not seem to be clear-cut answers.

Many who read this book will have some of their myths of prisons dispelled, see I was humbled by my work, and realize that although I come to conclusions I am still searching for answers. I hope my experiences will lead you, my readers, to ask questions too. I hope you tell your own stories, some from within your hearts and the confines of the prisons, and that you keep searching, for perhaps it's in the search itself that liberating truth is found. As the French writer André Gide said, "Believe those who are seeking the truth, but doubt those who find it."

1

Fear and Safety

"When I am afraid, I will trust in you."

—PSALM 56:3

PEOPLE OFTEN ASK ME if I was afraid working in the prisons. I wasn't. Did I see the prisoners or work directly with them? I saw prisoners and spoke with them almost daily once I began working in the prisons. They were not usually the cause of my fears. But I did begin praying on my drive to work—with my eyes open. During my career I traveled on Michigan roads south to Coldwater and Jackson, north to St. Louis, east to Ypsilanti, and west to Ionia—about an hour's drive to whatever prison and job I held. I had time to pray, but it wasn't by any means always for safety that I prayed, my own or others'.

I spent my childhood on a small dairy farm in the northwest corner of the state of Washington, a few miles south of the Canadian border. My parents' old-fashioned farm was a modest forty acres, with pastures separated by fences, a stand of cedars, and a marsh to the west of the barn and house. Deer drank in a pond, sharing it with the cows when they grazed in the back corner of the field. My sisters and I played in the woods among the cedars. At night in the spring we went to sleep hearing loud frog choruses from the swamps. Today I hear about fears of nature—plants, bugs, and animals—and read that we avoid forests because of our worries about the "wild," or what's left of it. Or perhaps we sit in front of computers and TVs, and miss the real outdoors show.

After September 11, 2001, fear became more politicized and danger took on colors and degrees of high and medium alert. Danger seemed pervasive, and rarely low. Now we fear losing our identity, health, money, youth, and beauty. We are especially afraid of dying. Incidents on planes drive some to near hysteria. Americans have been hijacked by fear.

Fear is personal and individual too. Before I worked in prisons, I worked at the University of Michigan in Ann Arbor. One evening as I climbed the stairs in the parking lot on the way to my car, a man in a ski mask exposed himself to me in the stairwell. I was terrified, sucked in my breath, and screamed, the reaction he likely expected and perhaps desired. After I reported the incident, I did not want to go back to the parking lot so a security guard walked me to my car that evening and every dark evening. I know what it means to be afraid of the shadows, or of being alone when you hear the creak on the stairs or see your cat look- ing intently at something you can't see. I'm constantly locking doors. More than once I locked my husband, Clay, out of the house when he was working a short distance away in the yard. Long before I worked in prisons, I locked doors without thinking, lest an intruder break in.

I live in a beautiful urban neighborhood. Large maple and oak trees adorn our yard, and the Grand River flowing east marks the northern boundary of our yard. It's easy to be complacent here.

One summer afternoon, I heard a knock on my unlocked screen door. A young man of slight build with rusty colored hair stood there on my patio with a flat box in his arms. He launched into a frenetic sales pitch assuring me he'd give me a good deal on the box of meat he was selling since he was at the end of his delivery, and wanted to get rid of it. His clear grey eyes darted like small lizards from my face to the kitchen behind me with intensity. I turned my head to sneeze and blow my nose, and suddenly he was on the other side of the screen door in my kitchen. I couldn't scream. I seemed to be as frozen as the meat in the box he held. I fumbled for my purse and grabbed for some money inside it. The meat cost me little in terms of money. Once he left, and I could breathe again, I placed the box of meat in the freezer where it stayed for a long time before I threw it out. The meat was tainted with fear.

You can't work in a prison and avoid thinking about safety. We read the papers and files of prisoners who have committed violent acts. Ted Conover in his book *Newjack* says his experience as a corrections officer at Sing Sing in New York, was permeated with fear.[1] He writes about be- ing trained and filled up with rules, but having little knowledge of doing

1. Conover, *Newjack*, 95.

the job before he walked out on the block. He describes the dilemma of being a new officer as "the state certifying us as lion tamers before ever leaving us alone in a cage with a lion."[2] He writes about fears of screwing up, getting hurt, and generally being dehumanized. Working in close proximity to some prisoners can be difficult.

We can be consumed with fear, and it can diminish us, as Max Lucado, the Christian writer, reminds us:

> Fear, it seems, has taken up a hundred year lease on the building next door and set up shop. Oversized and rude, fear refuses to share the heart with anyone else, especially happiness. Did you ever see fear and happiness in the same heart? Did you ever see fear and hope in the same heart? Can anyone be clear thinking and afraid? Confident and afraid? Merciful and afraid? No. Fear is the big bully in the high school hallway, brash, loud, and unproductive. For all the noise fear makes, fear does little good. Fear never wrote a symphony. Fear never wrote a poem. Fear never negotiated a peace treaty. Fear never led a city out of bigotry or a nation out of poverty.
>
> Courage did. Hope did. Faith did. Fear? Fear does nothing good. Fear walks us into a prison and locks the door. Wouldn't it be great to walk out?[3]

Lucado uses a prison as a metaphor for what we allow fear to do to us, noting we can imprison ourselves with irrational fear.

Of course some degree of fear is healthy. Fear can protect us from actual dangers. One summer I climbed a glacier mountain. Our "team" prepared. We had the equipment we'd need including crampons, ice axes, and flashlights. We wore the latest warm, lightweight clothes, and were roped together to two guides who helped us avoid crevasses. I was vividly aware of the dangers: fogs, and avalanches, falling into an abyss, getting altitude sickness. When we began our ascent, fear, not coffee at 3 a.m., motivated me. We were elated when we made it up and then down safely again. Preparation for climbing the mountain prepared us.

Training and preparation for working in prisons protects those of us working there. In prisons employees often work together rather than in isolated areas, unless they are assigned to areas removed from prisoners in stations like towers. Prisons are like small towns. Most of the

2. Ibid., 69–70.

3. Lucado, *Fearless*, 5.

time, someone knows where you are, or can locate you by sending out radio communications. Corrections employees, responsible for controlling inmates sentenced to prisons, are good at what they do, and prisons function most of the time like clockwork, in routines.

In addition to the daily routines, prisons today are more prepared than in the past for violence when it erupts. Most prisons are not as large as Sing Sing, where Ted Conover worked. Movement is controlled. (Sixteen hundred inmates are not allowed recreation at the same time, as Conover alleges occurred at Sing Sing.)[4] Employees are trained to watch for signs of disturbances and either work to prevent them or diffuse them when they occur. Prisons have sound locking systems, personal protection devices and key control, and some have armed officers in towers and emergency response teams. The technology is increasingly sophisticated. If employees are alert and conduct shakedowns, it's harder for prisoners to hide weapons or contraband. In addition, prisoners who've committed some of the more serious crimes, those who will be in prison for some time, have an interest in a stable environment and are not necessarily those who are management problems.

Even with all these conditions and systems, training, and preparation, no prison can fortify itself completely against critical incidents. Corrections Officers, other employees, and prisoners and their families have different fears, but prisons are fear-charged environments where mistakes can be costly.

Prisoner escapes, suicides, riots, and hostage-taking incidents can occur regardless of how prepared employees are. I feared someone could be hurt or killed because I or someone I supervised overlooked something important and made a fatal mistake. When I was on duty, I carried a pager so employees at the prison could reach me for emergencies. I soon began to feel the vibration of the pager on my waist even when I wasn't being paged. Fear is real even when it's irrational.

Danger is not limited to a location like prison or a group of people like prisoners. People working on high ladders, doctors operating in emergency settings or sensitive surgeries, school teachers with unruly students and soldiers going to war all may have as much or more to fear as people working in prisons. Safety can't be pinned down to certain jobs or neighborhoods. What to do? We can enjoy the careers and lives

---

4. Conover, *Newjack*, 61.

we choose to live with inherent risks or never take any chances and be comfortable.

A few years ago my husband Clay and I went to Nigeria with a team of people from our church to partner with churches there working on the HIV/AIDS crisis. Our Nigerian colleagues and friends were always with us as we traveled from Abuja to Jos and surrounding regions. But we were stopped many times at checkpoints by young men with AK 47s. I lost track of which were military and police uniforms, not always realizing who they represented. But others without uniform were engaged in highway robbery.

One day as we were traveling to the Mkar region, young men tried to "nail board" us. They suddenly appeared from the woods on the road in front of us with boards full of nails to puncture our tires and stop the car so they could rob us. Our friend John was driving and swerved. I'd heard a board cracking, but thought we had escaped with our tires intact. Down the road fifteen minutes, our tires deflated. We stayed in a village we knew nothing about while some of our leaders traveled to a neighboring town to have the tires repaired. Dangerous, but we were on a mission and with friends which may have given us the illusion of safety. Later, when we traveled on, I watched the sides of the roads for men with boards.

About the time I began working in a prison, I had a few experiences that made me realize how elusive safety is. I couldn't tell prisoners or their parents not to be afraid, but I know I've often felt more frightened walking in dark parking lots than making rounds in a prison yard or housing unit at night. I think my fears made me understand employees, prisoners, and prisoners' families in ways I wouldn't have if I'd lived without any fear myself. I know many employees and prisoners and their families who fear and trust, trust and fear, and that we go through life often dancing between fear and safety, praying "When I am afraid, I will trust you."

2

Elusive Safety

"Everything turns to ashes in front of fear."

—ALBERT CAMUS, *CALIGULA*

A MOTHER'S FEAR

THE CAPTAIN SAID WHEN I walked in the door, "You have a phone call from the outside."

The mother of a prisoner who had contacted me waited for some reassurance. I always received more calls from prisoners' families on Monday. Weekend security staff waited for administrative staff who returned on Monday to make decisions about transfers and to sign records and they preferred that we talk with prisoners' families too.

A morning requiring multitasking was not unusual on Monday. The scheduled big transfer of prisoners to the Reformatory was also on the agenda. The Prison Reception Center was full, and I wanted to make sure all the transfer orders were signed. We couldn't have prisoners rejected at other prisons because their transfer orders didn't have the Deputy Warden's signature. We were desperate for the beds.

I recalled the conversation I had with a young prisoner on the list to go to the Reformatory. "And what are you in here for?" I knew it was for first-degree murder. He had pleaded with me not to send him to the Reformatory, although it was the prison where we sent young offenders who had committed serious crimes. "Why not?" I'd asked.

"It's the gladiator school....very dangerous," he said, shaking his head. I thought about the article, "Welcome to Gladiator School" about the division to which young convicted men were sentenced in the Cook County jail (Illinois), a place that Laurence Gonzales viewed as a training ground for warriors, a place where civilized norms were suspended.[1] Prisoners perpetuated the "gladiator" term for the Reformatory and frightened themselves about the unknown. The officers didn't always discourage the use of the term either, as though the shock of being in prison wasn't enough for the young men.

But the mother of the young prisoner waited on the phone.

"I haven't been able to visit him. He says he can't call me until he is approved to use the phone," said the prisoner's mother. The few telephones and other restrictions resulted in more calls like this from concerned family. Telephone conversations were a way to monitor the prisoners, though it took more of the employees' time. "I heard they all shower together," the mother continued.

I had spoken with her before, or someone like her, maybe another mother who had called because she had heard what can happen in prison. They know about sexual assaults even if their sons don't say anything. They don't raise the issue of rape as though saying the r-word could make it happen. Shame kept male rape from being reported. Some inmates were reluctant to report it and be labeled snitches. We had more training and rules in place. Rape in a prison, usually about domination and power, frightened young offenders, especially those of slight build. They knew they could become older, stronger prisoners' "punks." It was another reason I preferred sending the younger prisoners and those who were smaller or appeared effeminate to the Reformatory.

The Prison Rape Elimination Act of 2003 which charged the Bureau of Justice Statistics with undertaking surveys, also created the National Prison Rape Elimination Commission, whose mandate was to study the problem of rape and develop standards for the detection, prevention, and responses to the problem. In the March 25, 2010 issue of The New York Review of Books, David Kaiser and Lovisa Stannow, in their article, "The Way to Stop Prison Rape," report that the number of those sexually abused behind bars every year is far more than 100,000, and that the abuse is usually perpetrated not by other inmates but by members of the prison staff. They also report a reduction of incidents of sexual abuse in some facilities because of policies and practices, and common sense measures like the training and monitoring of staff. The Justice

1. Gonzales, "Welcome to Gladiator School," 34.

Department is looking at "corrections systems already implementing the standards including Macomb County Sheriff's Department in Michigan which has a medium-sized jail for men and women to help them achieve standards even before they are legally obliged to do so." One of the standards requires that inmates be classified and screened to assess their risk of being sexually abused by other inmates. [2]

"There are officers monitoring and observing the showers," I tell the anxious mother.

"And they go to the yard together? Are there assaults?" she asks.

She was right, of course. Any time prisoners are together, there is a chance of fights or assaults. She was not accusing us of anything. She was reasonable and afraid for her son. She wanted me to say it wouldn't happen. "We *observe* (observe is better than watch, and we can't watch everyone all the time) the prisoners when they are in contact with one another, and we don't allow the most violent prisoners out of their cells to mix with others," I said, though prisoners with violent pasts weren't always the only ones who assaulted someone in prison.

"They told him he'd be in there a month before going to another prison," she said.

All the young males sentenced to prison go to the Reception Center first. The information gathered is used to separate them into security levels and send them to prisons ranging from minimum security for short sentences to maximum security for those who commit serious crimes and have more time. Few go directly to the one super maximum security prison in the system which is reserved for prisoners who are difficult to control at other prisons or those with horrendous, notorious, or highly publicized crimes like killing a police officer.

I told the mother that prison employees were collecting information on her son's background, criminal history, and determining what type of risk he might be, before classifying and transferring him to a prison. "What is he in here for, and how long is his sentence?" I asked. I knew her response would give me a good idea of what security level he was and where he would be transferred.

"He assaulted someone. The report made him sound terrible, but he's only twenty-two, and it's not like he's a bad kid. They made him out to be this horrible person."

---

2. Kaiser and Stannow, "Prison Rape and the Government," 26–28.

I imagined what the son's record would say. Usually there is some history of offenses or serious crime before a judge would sentence a young man to prison. His victim may have required medical attention or hospitalization. The charge was likely "Assault to do Great Bodily Harm."

"Our family is solid. His sister is in college and gets very good grades. We don't know what happened to him."

Even if his record with all the accumulated facts was in front of me, I wouldn't know how to respond to this. What she meant by "what happened to him" was that he was in prison, and not what happened before that. She didn't talk about how he had gradually gotten into trouble and the path that had led here.

"At first, he was in a unit that was modern, and now they've moved him to another one. It isn't clean. He said they've seen mice. The food isn't always hot either. When he complained one of the guards said, 'I'm sorry that you don't like our hotel accommodations.'"

Familiar with our system, I knew he'd been placed in the older unit because his "processing" was complete, and he was ready to be transferred to the prison at his security level and waiting for a bed.

Again I tried to assure her. "He won't be in the older unit long, and he'll be transferred soon."

"What if something happens? How do I know he's safe in there?"

This was the question she'd been asking all along. Being sentenced to prison does not automatically put a person in danger. There is not a "before" when you were safe, and an "after" when you are no longer safe, like stepping into the deep end of a pool. There are dangers, but most prisoners suffer from the slow corrosiveness of monotony, which seeps into their institutionalized lives like the humidity that rusts the pipes in the old prisons. Months of being told when to eat, go to school or work, sleep, and take count robs prisoners of their youth and their freedom to make choices—even the wrong choices. No one coming in knows that yet. Age lines in their faces replace bruises of younger pugnacious men, mark them doing their own time, walking straight ahead, and living in the prison's times and schedules. As Gonzales said some time ago, "I know now that if a man hasn't lost his soul when he commits his crime, he's at high risk of losing it when he serves his sentence."[3]

---

3. Gonzales, "Welcome to Gladiator School," 40.

THE SCARE

The mother's fears about her son, and the prisoner's fears about transferring to the Reformatory reminded me of what happened to me the night before starting work at the Huron Valley Men's Maximum Security prison. I traveled the hour to Ypsilanti and the Harbor Cove studio apartment that I rented ten minutes' drive from the prison. I arrived there around 10:00 p.m. and began moving a few things into the apartment.

On one trip from my car I opened the door to set a box on the landing, and a man and woman screaming from the sidewalk, burst out of the darkness and into my apartment.

"He has a knife! He's going to kill us," they cried.

Panicked, I screamed back. In defense of the assault I thought awaited me, I said, "You can't come in here. I'll call the police."

"We can't leave. He'll kill us."

"Who?" I asked, still terrified.

"We picked him up from the airport. He is a friend of hers," said the man breathlessly. "We were having dinner, and he became jealous and angry. All of a sudden he grabbed a knife from the drawer and said he'd kill us!"

Maybe they'd tried this before—a set-up, and they'd rob me. I wasn't naïve. The abruptness of the break-in stunned me. Only a desire to rob me or fear could have given them that kind of speed and force. Mercifully for me, it was fear. The police arrived quickly and told them what I had already told them—that they couldn't stay in my apartment.

I'm sure many of the occupants of Harbor Cove saw the flashing lights of the police car rotating in their windows and lighting up their walls. The school principal who worked at the prison lived there too, and word about the police at the new employee's apartment spread quickly. The next day he stood in my office with an amused look. "Ours was a nice neighborhood until you moved in."

In fact it was a nice neighborhood. That evening, I looked at Ford Lake outside the sliding glass doors of the apartment, quiet and calm. Two boys tossed a softball back and forth on the lawn by the lake. Both "Harbor" and "Cove" seemed to speak of safety. No one walking by on the sidewalk that day would see any evidence of a break-in of my apartment by the couple the night before. They had not robbed or assaulted me. Only their screams ripping through the silence, and their intrusion in my apartment threw me off balance. Violence can creep into nice neighborhoods. Even gated communities are not immune from those whose criminal behavior sends them on to another gated community—a prison.

NO GUARANTEES

The mother of the young prisoner was waiting on the phone for word of his safety.

"There are no guarantees, but we work hard to keep everyone safe," I said. I wanted to ask if her son was safe on the streets before he came to prison. Was he safe when he was committing crimes or assaulting others? Were others safe from him in the community? She was not ready to hang up because she was not satisfied that we could protect her son.

I want to make it right for her, but she wants something from me that I can't give her. I want her son to make it, and make it right. We end the conversation somehow, her voice full of anxiety and hope. I promise to check on him. He may have been a hellion on the street. Now it is our obligation to protect him.

A year later I walk through the prison yard making my rounds as the setting sun leaves a rosy color in the western sky. "Hello, Deputy Libolt," yells one of the inmates on the court as he shoots a basket. I'm ready to go home.

I'm in a routine passing through the three gates, used to hearing the familiar metal of each, detecting little differences in the way each one sounds as they slide closed. I sign out in the logbook as I always do. Prison officers at every station, like angels, know where I am. I walk through the dark parking lot towards my car and lock my doors. Glancing over my shoulder at the prison lights in my rearview mirror, I drive to my apartment.

The short walk from the parking lot into my apartment is the hardest. I open the door and turn on the light before locking it behind me, thinking of scenes from too many movies where good guys are heroic and ladies are rescued and live, at the end. But I know sons of concerned mothers sometime wait in the dark to attack women like me, as desperate as the mother who called me.

3

Call Me Crazy

"When we remember we are all mad,
the mysteries disappear and life stands explained."
—MARK TWAIN, NOTEBOOK

WHEN I DRIVE UP, it's dark, but Jay is easy to spot. He's an imposing figure standing in the light from Themmos, the bright restaurant where he can get a small amount of food cheaply and stay in the restaurant's warmth a long time. When he looked for a suit at Goodwill for the few occasions, like church, for which he thought he needed one, he had difficulty finding one that would fit his large frame. Jay lifted weights when he was younger, but years of unemployment and inactivity have all had an impact, and he has less definition and strength than before. When he rides with me, he must move the seat as far back as it will go to squeeze in. He wears a lumpy, disheveled brown jacket and, for a big guy, takes small, slow steps as though he is carrying a sack of potatoes. He has the duffle bag he carries with him wherever he goes.

When I see him, I give my horn a toot, but he looks at me as though I am crazy. I answered the phone when he called for a ride, but he resents his dependence. His face is at an angle, both surprised and frowning with an underlying expression of pain, accentuated by age settling into facial cracks and lines. His moods swing depending on what medication he's supposed to be on and how often he has the money to buy it. He vacillates between giddiness and sullen silence. I'm often trapped between my irritation with his temporary hilarity and pity for the misery oozing from his silence.

When he's high, he tells blonde jokes that make me cringe and then he laughs like a twelve year old, often punching me in the arm. "What do you call a smart blonde? A golden retriever. What did the blonde say when she found out she was pregnant? Are you sure it's mine?" At other times his quiet brooding makes the twenty minute ride to his apartment seem endless. When he finds some equilibrium from either extreme, he talks about politics, popular physics, and music.

He has called me tonight because he's hearing voices. I didn't expect the call on a wintry Sunday night, and with the background noise from the restaurant I had to ask him to repeat what he'd said. He raised his voice above the din. "I'm hearing voices, and need a ride home. I thought I could handle it, but I can't."

"I'm in the middle of making dinner so I won't be able to come right now," I said as I stirred the mixture for a new pasta dish in the frying pan, and wondered if he could tell the voices to wait.

I worked as a Deputy Warden in a prison that housed mentally ill prisoners and had professionals working with them, and I am familiar with the peculiarities of hearing voices. I remembered the prisoner who recently couldn't sleep because of the voices. His bed was alive, and talking to him. Officers moved the mattress from his cell. It's relatively easy to remove something tangible, less so to relieve the psychic pain.

"Well, I'm not going anywhere. I'll be here."

There is no bus transportation on Sunday evenings. When he's too far from home to walk, he calls either my husband or me. Each time he moves to another public housing project farther south and farther from downtown (and where we live), he spends more time riding. Even if the buses were running he would be unlikely to ride one after a recent incident. His morose look and size can have an intimidating effect on the other passengers who ride the bus. Recently, he defended a fellow passenger, but in so doing offended the bus driver and the remaining passengers. While some passengers might become hostile or defensive, he is only trying to be helpful or good in the way he knows, and sees himself as a miserable failure if there is a negative reaction. He doesn't intend to be a troublemaker, but one thing leads to another, and inadvertently he can cross the line from the pleasant and acceptable to the irritating and threatening. The ensuing criticism crushes him.

The recipe I was trying was new, and it was better to finish the dish rather than interrupt it at this stage. I boiled the pasta a few more minutes, drained it, added the ricotta, mozzarella, and Parmesan so they could melt in the pasta before adding the spices, raisins, and chopped cauliflower/spinach mixture in the frying pan. It would be good, but too rich to eat often.

Jay didn't mind waiting. It was not as though he'd be going to work the next day. Some assumed that a strapping man could hold a job, but he could not. He couldn't work as a parking attendant or at an automated car wash for more than a morning before some customer would get on his nerves and cause him stress. He had been successful a few years ago when he held a job driving a van of other mentally ill and disabled patients to their appointments. He loved to drive, and we heard little from him. The job was one of the best medications in a string of drugs ending in "il" like "Elavil" that had been prescribed for him throughout the years. But with a new administration, the job fizzled out along with funding for the mentally ill.

Another unfortunate incident for Jay occurred when there was a crackdown on deadbeat dads. The newspapers had reported the sad stories of families who couldn't make ends meet because of dads unwilling or unable to support their kids. Such a crackdown looked fair enough on paper unless you knew that it wouldn't work for Jay who had a disability and could not support his child if he'd wanted to. It looked good until you knew that some dads, like a number of moms, fall through the cracks. At a time when many professionals are increasingly critical of incarcerating mentally ill offenders, Jay was placed in jail as a deadbeat dad. Once the courts realized he was disabled and an error had been made, he was released and stranded without transportation over an hour's drive away. His pastor brought him back to town.

Judge Steven Leifman of Miami-Dade County reports that ninety per cent of the country's hospital beds for the mentally ill have been closed, and the nation has experienced a 400 percent increase in the mentally ill offenders entering the criminal justice system. The report in *Corrections Today* April 2009 indicates there are 500,000 people with mental illness in the nation's prisons and jails, and another 500,000 on probation. [1]

I turned off the burner, set a lid on the pasta, and grabbed a coat. The drive across town doesn't take long. No lights are on in office buildings. People seem to be in their homes on this cold Sunday evening.

1. Leifman, "Leifman Advocates for the Mentally Ill," 77.

As Jay makes his way to my car, it is hard for me to gauge his mood. I get ready for him to put the passenger seat as far back as it will go, but instead he pulls the back door open and tosses his duffle bag on the back seat and slides in beside it. I look back in his direction.

"You can sit in the front," I tell him.

He doesn't sound sad but resigned and somehow, satisfied.

"No, I don't want to be near anybody when I'm hearing voices." Perhaps he's glad for the company. The price for isolation and loneliness may keep him out of conflict and make him susceptible to hearing voices. His smoky breath is short, and he's wheezing. I am already driving down Pine Avenue when he says, "They're telling me to kill people." I want to tell him, *Get out of my car.* If some voice is telling him to kill me, I wish he'd keep it to himself. Better to be stabbed or shot from the back. I don't want to see it coming. I imagine the newspaper headlines. "Deputy Warden picks up Mentally Ill Man Who Hears Voices." But why are these kinds of voices malevolent? Do they ever say pleasant things like, "I hope you're having a nice day, or "You're looking good?" How about, "I'm ok and you're not so bad either?" Better yet, could I have a voice telling him, "Don't kill her? I'm from outside. I'm not anyone from your tortured past stirring up all the pain that has become a part of you."

I wondered if these terrible voices took hold like the strange story of the demon-possessed man in three gospels of the Bible (Matthew 8, Luke 8, and Mark 5.) So full of anguish, he approached Jesus and begged him not to harm him. When Jesus commanded the evil spirits to come out of the man, the strange story tells us that they asked to go into a herd of swine on a hillside, and Jesus gave them permission to flee and reside in the pigs. Now we look to professionals, and it may take years to cure someone. Perhaps there are too few herds of pigs on hillsides into which evil spirits can go. But I longed for one of those mental health professionals right now!

"You're very angry?" I hear my voice come from some restrained place, the words barely coming from my tightened throat.

"Yes, I could just kill. It's rage." *When I am afraid, I will trust in you.* I pray that I'll keep my wits about me. I even drive the speed limit. I can't imagine that he'd have a gun or knife. Jay has never been violent and considers me a friend. He rides with me to church, and turns his anger inward. I try to think of prison policies that would apply in these circumstances, but they don't come to me now, and there are no professionals here to consult. I know that some of the errors we make in the prison during emergencies are related to acting out of instinct instead of following policy. Sometimes there is dissonance between what prison policy says and instinct, an estrangement between actions and requirements.

"Are you taking your medication?" I ask.

"I see the doctor tomorrow. They're re-opening my case." Depending on the doctor, his case is open or somewhat closed. In Community Mental Health he is assigned on-call doctors who are available but may not know him. They see the facts in his file, and occasionally there is a new diagnosis for the same maladies. He is relieved he will be seen, and the last few years as medications have become more appropriate his suicide attempts have become more rare. His talking is a good sign.

"Stop! Don't," he says as I slow down, and then, "I'm not talking to you. There are two people, men, and sometimes they want me to join them." He sighs and says as though he realizes his effect on me, "Everyone at the church would just like me to disappear. So would you."

It's true. Few people from church want to be with him for long. The last time he attended a class at church, he tried to steer the discussion away from the topic, and then accused the annoyed leader of being defensive, while she and others redirected the discussion back. By the time I picked him up, he was deflated about what had taken place. The dark could not hide the disappointment that hung on his frame like the smoke that clings to his clothes. I asked what was wrong, though I knew from past attempts on his part to connect with others that his participation had likely been unsuccessful, and he was taking it hard. I tried to find out what had happened in the class, but the conversation was over, much like the time I had asked him about his childhood. Each answer to my next question was shorter until he said that he didn't want to talk about it. Tonight I detect a lift in his voice, and he is almost cheerful.

"Is the church still collecting books to raise money for new ones?" he asks. He has a bag of books if I will take them. "I'd like to contribute something, and not always be taking." And then, as he remembered the others, "Don't bother me," to the voices. "Can you drop me off at the Carter Drop-In Center on Cherry and Grant?" he asks.

"What is it?" I ask.

"It's a place to hang out, you know, for 'crazies.'" He laughs. "We're all crazy there." I drive there and stop across from the building, and he climbs out of the backseat and picks up the duffle bag. "Thanks," he says, and walks toward the building.

Acting "crazy" is a way to connect. Tonight he is better than when he is too high and giddy or so low he's not talking, but I've not seen him psychotic. Still, when he gets out of the car, I want to say, "The next time you are hearing voices, don't call me. I'll call you," and I'm relieved that the only voices I hear are on the radio.

It could have been different. Sometimes acting "crazy" is an attempt to make contact. We hear voices that tell us to leave comfort, our food, and what is warm, and answer calls to a different part of the world where someone on the margins—poor, lonely or inadequate—waits, and we step into their crazy world because we are needed. We may be scared. It may be risky. But most of the time it is just an inconvenience. We may know there will be no reciprocity, no rewards for what we do except that someone waits for us. One person may depend on us to keep them sane, and we are relieved that we were not hurt. We helped someone and for a few minutes we think that people are crazier than we are. Crazy spirits can be driven out in a single car ride even in a city in which no swine are in sight. And that can be comforting in ways that surpass good pasta.

4

Blood on the Sidewalk

"In the face of the moral hierarchies suggested to us by human standards of discrimination, by the differences so obvious between us upright citizens and the murderers, rapists, thieves, and cheats who fill our prisons, it is an ongoing task of Christian education to keep ourselves aware of our full membership in the universal brotherhood of miscreants."

—ROBERT C. ROBERTS [1]

"Brothers and sisters, if someone is caught in a sin, you who live by the Spirit should restore that person gently. But watch yourselves, or you also may be tempted."

— GALATIANS 6:1

I WAS NOT SHOCKED to see blood on the sidewalk. I was walking with the Warden in the Huron Valley Maximum Security Facility for men. I had come from Central Office in Lansing where I worked in program evaluation, but I had heard about critical incidents in prisons. As an administrator, I was new to prison work. I expected to see some blood. On this particular day, we saw the drops of blood that remained and then what looked like a smear where someone may have fallen. A prisoner had been stabbed.

Rick, a well-spoken prisoner in khaki pants and a pressed shirt, (at that time prisoners did not wear uniforms), approached the Warden and asked if the blood on the sidewalk could be cleaned up. Rick was a

1. Roberts, *Spirituality and Human Emotion*, 120.

prisoner representative and in this capacity had the Warden's attention more frequently than other prisoners.

The Warden, disgusted about the stabbing, turned to me, and said, "We'll leave it. It reminds all of us where we work." Then he added, "Always know who's behind you, around you, and in front of you, and what prisoners are capable of." Throughout my career in Michigan Corrections, I did not forget his advice.

Although the prisoners at Huron Valley differed from one another as much as any of us, they had in common their classification as maximum security, and we viewed them as a group regardless of whether they had committed one serious crime with a long sentence, or were habitual offenders, or management problems. We judged them by what type of a risk they were. We had to assume they were capable of behaving like the most dangerous residing among them.

Rick, who had spoken to the Warden, looked vaguely familiar. I'd seen him before. He had been in a prison in Marquette several years before when I was gathering data for evaluation research. Not long after the stabbing, I guided some visitors on a tour through the prison. They thought Rick was an employee. Prisoners like him could fool people. He was attentive and attractive—even classy looking. According to his record, in a rage he had killed several people in a card game. A man with good manners, poised, seemingly controlled—and a murderer.

I can't imagine committing a crime as serious as Rick's. Prisons are especially built to house those who have committed monstrous crimes and the higher a prisoner's security level was, the more distance from them there seemed to be. But I had worked long enough in the Michigan prisons to ask myself whether I could have committed *some* of the crimes the prisoners had. I wondered on my worst days how different I was from some of those locked up, and I struggled with questions about justice.

In my capacity as Deputy Warden I reviewed background checks on employees who were trained to use weapons, something I did through the Law Enforcement Information Network or, LEINS. Some of these employees had records of contact with the police. A few of our employees had even served time in prisons. In fact, on taking a position at one prison I found an investigation file left in my desk drawer—an investigation of a felony of an employee who was a supervisor. Either his bosses had not wished to pursue it, or it wouldn't have stood up to scrutiny in the courts, or perhaps he was innocent. Later, the supervisor, who was the subject of the investigation, was sentenced to prison for another offense.

One evening, a promising young man who was drinking killed another person while driving home. It's a story we hear about in the news frequently. He had never committed a crime before, but one action and a lost life placed him in the same prison as a person for whom crime had become a way of life. He must have asked himself many times why he drank, or why that car came into his path that evening. Alcohol and drugs alter our judgment, and we do things we'd never do if we weren't under their influence.

Last year the local newspaper reported that a man couldn't believe he'd murdered his wife of many years. If he'd not had the gun, she might be living today. Thinking about killing someone can quickly become a reality when one has access to a gun. Another article tells of a desperate woman who over a long period regularly took small amounts of money from her employer until she was convicted of fraud. Prominent sports figures, celebrities, and priests are frequently in the papers, guilty of various offenses. Crimes vary in their gravity and offenders are handled in various ways in court. Some offenses receive stiff penalties and others are handled as though they were merely serious pranks.

Before I worked for the Department of Corrections, I worked at a youth training facility where the young men talked about their past crimes in a group. One of the boys from a town in northern Michigan had to "tell" the group the story of his crime. He was serving time in the youth facility because he had stolen money from parking meters. Some of the young men from large cities laughed. "Say what?" Their crimes were far more serious, and they saw the northern boy as naïve and his parking meter thefts as petty. Because of limited resources, police may be handling only the worst crimes in urban areas while in more rural areas, those committing crimes of all types are well known and receive more attention with less tolerance on the part of judges.

We know that sometimes one justice system is applied to the wealthy, educated, and those committing white-collar crimes, and another to minorities and the poor. Offenders living in a middle-class neighborhood, who have money for good attorneys, or who are privileged in another way may not go to prison, while the poor and minorities committing similar offenses do. Some offenders live a life of accumulating crime while others, like the young man who was drunk and killed someone on the highway, commit only one life-stopping offense.

The line between those within prisons and those outside is not as clear as fortified walls or steel bars make it seem. Sometimes the lines are as blurred and messy as blood on the sidewalk.

A friend tells of having been with an attorney who said, "I could never kill anyone." My friend knew it wasn't true—of either one of them. She'd lived in the inner city of Detroit and had planned at one time to kill her mother's abusive boyfriend by dropping a large rock on his head as he walked through the door of their apartment. He didn't come home that night, and that may have saved both of them, him from death and her from a murder charge.

Perhaps you believe like the attorney talking with my friend that you could never kill anyone. Maybe you've done nothing more seriously wrong than scarf up a few grapes from the produce section in the grocery store or taken a pen from a hotel, and believe that you could not be sentenced for a serious crime. The man who had the gun and killed his wife, and a woman stealing small sums of money know how quickly that line is crossed. They are also acutely aware of how much grief they have caused.

Some issues haunted me. Could I have done what that prisoner who took small amounts of money from her employer did? Could I have been sentenced? Was her sentence just? Do we let white collar property offenders off easy while desperate poor people serve time? Are financiers living high off Wall Street as responsible for harm as small time thieves? Do we know how much harm we cause though we may not have committed a crime? Is that prisoner innocent as he claims? Are all of us capable of crime? Is the only difference between us that some of us believe we won't be caught?

When I first began working at the maximum security prison where I saw the blood on the sidewalk, a Deputy Warden and Warden tricked me. I'm sure I appeared naïve with my questions. They called me to the Warden's office. They looked serious when I walked in, and placed handcuffs on me. They explained that there were reports I was smuggling in drugs. I was too shocked to ask who reported me, or if they had a credible source. I remember stammering out, "There's a mistake. I wouldn't do that." Fortunately, the Warden couldn't make eye contact or keep a straight face, and finally he and the deputy both burst out laughing. They told me that I was about the last person they'd ever suspect of smuggling in drugs. But for weeks I thought about the prank.

What if the source had been believable? What if they had set me up, or planted evidence? How difficult would that be? I never forgot the Warden's words that day on the sidewalk. *"Always know who's behind you, around you, and in front of you, and what prisoners are capable of."* Staff too, I thought.

That day when a prisoner was stabbed, an officer had tried to intervene, and he was also stabbed. He didn't realize it until another officer told him, and pulled him away from the fray. The Warden wanted the blood left on the sidewalk. We didn't know whose blood it was—prisoners' or employees', maybe both comingling—staying there until a rain washed it away.

When I try making too many distinctions between prisoners and those who have not been in prison, I find myself in messy territory. Drawing too many lines between us is problematic. Like the Warden said, *blood on the sidewalk reminds us all of where we work*—and of who we are, where we live, and what we can expect. Rick, who asked the Warden if the blood could be cleaned off the sidewalk because it wasn't seemly, has more than one life sentence for violent crimes. Though he's not likely to be released from prison to the community, most prisoners will go on parole or be discharged, and live in our neighborhoods and communities.

We are related, not as blood brothers and sisters, but as sharing a common humanity and community. We are in life together. It is why we can't isolate ourselves, why it is to our mutual benefit to assist prisoners when they return to our communities.

Long before I worked in the prisons, I knew I wanted to work with those who struggled, or were damaged, people who had on-going problems. As ill-equipped as I was to solve their problems, I didn't want to escape to where life was easy or comfortable. I was raised on a Jesus who hung around the poor, the sick, the mentally ill, and others on the margins. A hymn I remember had these words, "What can wash my sin away? Nothing but the blood of Jesus." As my pastor husband says, we don't like to sing the "blood" songs anymore. They're not nice. We prefer a more sanitized, antiseptic Jesus, a Jesus who is spiritual, and less physical. We forget about Jesus eating bread and dying a messy death. We don't want to look at blood. But God cares about the bloodiness of life, and lingers where life is messy—in wars, abuse, family conflicts, sickness, and prisons. The God of monthly periods, childbirth, fistula, and gunshot wounds is not far from us. Suffering is the way of the Cross. God is in places like prisons that cry out for mercy and justice.

Prisoners keep me from becoming smug. Being with them reminds me how even with all the advantages of a solid family, church, and education, I am vulnerable to being accused of a crime and to committing one. Some of us working in the prisons know we are fortunate to go home at night. As Billy Sunday, said, "There but for the grace of God go I." Rain can't wash away the blood that sometimes spills onto the sidewalks.

5

Courting Justice

"ARE YOU ON YOUR way to the Fifth Courtroom too?" A young man with curly hair in blue jeans asked me.

I had hoped it wouldn't be so obvious. I was a deputy warden of a prison and had worn my no-nonsense navy suit, hoping nobody was going to recognize me here in court. I clicked along in my pumps and managed a tight "Yes," and said, "I think it's at the end of this hall."

I would not have had to go to court. I could have just paid my fine for speeding, but I, like everyone else here, believed that I had been unjustly accused and was appealing my case. I arrived early and sat with the twenty other scofflaws on hard, straight backed benches that allowed none of the slouching to which those of us accused of civil infractions were prone.

The young man sat next to me. We had passed through the new metal detector and boarded the same elevator to the fourth floor. He was nervous and talkative but in very good spirits.

"I took the same route to work on my motorcycle every day with police in the area, and the day I got the ticket, the cop said that I had 'rolled through' the stop sign."

On the other side of him an older man who wore a dirty t-shirt chimed in. "I drive a taxi and wasn't even on that street at the time I got the ticket." Hmm, only a technicality, I thought, and yet at the prison we lost what seemed like sure-fire cases on technicalities. Crossing a "t", and dotting an "i"—the details—were essential components of winning or at least not losing. The taxi driver went on to defend himself. "What do I have to lose by fighting it anyway? It's worth a try."

None of us was guilty, or so we thought, and we became more talkative. A feeling of "we're all in this together" permeated the room.

Perhaps it was a mistake placing us in the same room where mob mentality could take over. Perhaps committing a small civil infraction could lead to a rebellion or more serious law breaking.

A young black woman with two small children sat on the other side of me. I did not feel very friendly so I was relieved that she was quiet. I did not want to hear another excuse for breaking the law. I didn't want to admit that I was a deputy warden in a prison. I imagined eyebrows going up over even alleged minor violations. A deputy warden should be an example, and, like all examples, if I could violate the law, then…. For some, there would be the pleasure of knowing that an "enforcer" of the law was not above it and would be punished. But in prisons the line between employees and prisoners is not always so clear. Workers fall prey to temptation and become entangled in the law, hung by their own ropes.

We wanted to draw sharp distinctions between those who went home at night and those who had to stay—distinctions we continued to make long after judges ordered sentences for prisoners. One night my fellow officers amused themselves with a story about locking up another officer in an empty cell he was inspecting. Just that quick he went from working outside to being captured inside.

A female employee received a letter from a prisoner who saw a newspaper with her offense and her address. He wrote,

> "I guess you are wondering who I am, what do I want and how do I know you. I saw your sentencing for DUI (Driving Under the Influence) in the paper and I figure you could relate due to your little 'run-in' with the law. I am in need of a friend as I'm far from home. I've been locked up since last year for a parole violation of carrying a cell phone. I guess they figured I was going to reach out and touch someone, ha—smile. I'm handsome, 200 lbs. with brown hair and eyes. I have no children nor have I been married. If you think you might like to be friends, drop me a line and say or ask what comes to mind. A letter is always nice, especially from a beautiful woman."

No, I had no wish to discuss why I was in court. My explanations would have sounded less convincing than those of the men. I began to wonder what the authorities would grant in my appeal. True, there had been cars passing me on the highway before the officer on a motorcycle flagged me down, and I was the one going slowly enough for a motorcycle cop to catch. The drivers who passed should have received tickets, instead of going by smug in the knowledge that the law hadn't caught them. My appeal would sound feeble in comparison to the men's. I imagined the judge saying, paltry excuses. I might be reduced to whimpering "It's unfair," and begging for mercy. I remembered prisoners who talked about their crimes, using terminology like, "I caught a case" as though there were violations floating around like flu viruses. "Is that like catching a cold?" I would ask.

In the movie, *My Mother's Castle* by Marcel Pagnol, one of the characters is accused of trespassing. "You are so weak when you are so wrong," he's told. Perhaps like many prisoners, I'd appear weak and so wrong.

One of the little girls with the young woman next to me looked up and smiled. "I know a card trick. Pull out a card." I drew one from her deck. She shuffled the cards, but the trick didn't work. "Pull again." She practiced on me a few times, and occasionally drew the card that I had selected and kept secret, right out of the deck. I wondered if justice was ever like that. Prisoners often said of their violations, "I was in the wrong place at the wrong time." Would justice be like that too? Would one of us be selected to be guilty or not guilty, by the luck of the draw? Would the white man wearing the dirty t-shirt be lucky or the young black woman with the two little girls?

When I was in high school I dated a boy who took me to a carnival. We walked to the booth where we could win a fluffy teddy bear. All the boy had to do was shoot darts at a spinning target. "Close, just missed the target, and one more and another throw at fifty cents," yelled the man in charge. Every shot was costly, and by the time we had the teddy bear, we had paid for it. Rather than question the accuracy of his shots, we decided that the game was rigged.

The presiding magistrate walked into the room and took his position in an elevated chair. Five empty benches separated him from us, but he looked approachable. We were quiet. The taxi driver spoke up first. Where is the policeman who issued the tickets?"

"He may not make it here today," said the official.

The guy sitting next to me turned to me. "They are not paid for these hearings, and if they don't show, we walk."

I found my voice. "How often does that happen?"

"One officer didn't show up for one whole day of hearings last week," the magistrate said. I heard a hopeful hum rise up from our delinquent group. "If he doesn't show up, you're free to go, and your tickets will be dismissed."

We watched the clock, and hopeful anticipation grew into relief as we waited and no officer walked through the door. Even the magistrate seemed relieved. He called the court to order.

"I'll be calling your names and signing your citations." By this time we were talking and laughing. One pleasant-looking lady with a big blonde hairdo in the front row said, "God bless America," and turning to the person next to her asked rhetorically, "Aren't you glad you live in America?"

The magistrate began to call our names one by one, and as we filed to his desk he wrote something on each of our papers. I waited for him to call, "Leebolt" which is usually how "Libolt" is pronounced by strangers. He called a version of my first name, and I recognized it, and presented my request for the hearing to him. He signed it for my dismissal.

"But what about the money I paid for my fine?" I asked him.

"You paid? Never do that," he said and sent me to another line where I got my money back. I was free.

On my car radio there is a report about a man who worked as a bookstore clerk and had been reading something "questionable" and had appeared "nervous." Someone looking over his shoulder at what he was reading reported him, and the FBI subsequently questioned him. I missed where it had happened. Was it America?

I drove away from court with an eye on my speedometer.

STOPPED BY ANOTHER COP

A few years ago when I was on vacation in my hometown of Lynden, Washington, my mom and two sisters with me, I, behind the wheel of my rental car, went shopping at a mall an hour away. On our return home on I-5 close to Chuckanut Drive, I became aware of a cop car in my rearview mirror. I realized he was after me, so I pulled over to the side of the expressway, while trying to remember what traffic violation I had committed. I watched him, pen and pad in hand, walk to my car and peer in my window.

"So, where are you going?" he asked, sarcasm dripping from his mouth.

"North to Lynden," I said, "and I wasn't speeding."

"Oh, no." He said. "You weren't speeding. What do you think you were doing?"

I felt my face getting hot. I wanted to smack him. I wanted to say, I don't need to guess. Just tell me.

"You were switching lanes without signaling."

It must have been a slow day, or perhaps he'd had a fight with someone at work. He would go back to the station and tell his buddies how he stopped me and what he'd said. I could hear him say, 'You should have seen the look on her face when I said, "Oh no, you weren't speeding."'

He walked back to his car after giving me a warning. I was relieved I didn't get a ticket, but I felt guilty and wanted to clean the sarcasm out of my car. I worried that my mom and sisters would think I was negligent.

I've wondered if it was the talking. If I'd been alone and switched lanes without using my turn signal, would he have stopped me? Perhaps he didn't think we could drive safely while talking.

The officer who gave me the ticket that resulted in my court appearance gave it to me as though it was part of his job he didn't relish. The second officer gave me a warning with humiliation—a price, but nothing I had to fight in court.

I knew an officer who had been stabbed in prison disturbances several times, and yet delivered meals professionally to segregated prisoners almost daily. His warden reminded me that's what objectivity was—going in everyday and treating all the prisoners with respect.

6

Car Theft

I DON'T REMEMBER THE name of the play we had seen at the theater, only walking to the parking lot and discovering our car was missing. We stood in the parking lot in disbelief. The lot holds about a dozen cars at the most, and there was no large, burgundy Buick anywhere. Working in a prison as a deputy warden had not prepared me for being a victim of crime. These types of crimes were more likely to occur in large cities, but this was Lansing, Michigan, with a small downtown that was usually quiet at night. We walked back into the theatre. People felt sorry for us, asked if we had locked the doors (yes), and then offered to call the police. They came quickly and looked skeptical. Had the car been impounded? Had we made all of our payments? Yes, we had.

The next day we told two friends from the police department what had happened. One of them said, "It's probably been taken to a chop shop for its parts. You'll never see it again." The other one said, "Some gangs steal cars as part of their initiation rites. They ride around, get high, trash them and run the cars out of gas and then leave them on some street." Fortunately, it was the latter. Our car had been left on a street, and trashed, but it was recovered. We could hardly believe our luck. The tennis racket and sports bag were still in the trunk. The police had cleaned up the car the best they could, but it had taken a beating. It looked dingy and the steering wheel column had been damaged and was never quite the same. It had aged in the ways people do who take bad trips on drugs.

I don't know if the gang members were ever caught, but as Deputy Warden I watched prisoner records for some time after that to see if anyone had been sentenced for stealing a burgundy Buick.

I interviewed young male prisoners under the age of twenty-one who were sentenced to prison for the first time. They had committed a range of offenses, and when I read their records and interviewed them, I resisted the temptation to be judgmental. Sometimes I found myself asking, "Why?" and "What in the world?" There were the crimes that were boneheaded stupid mistakes and crimes in which people were seriously hurt. The crimes never stopped shocking me, but it was not my job to set anyone straight. Incoming prisoners had already seen a judge, and they stood before me simply so that I could tell them, from information in their records, what level of security risk they were, minimum, medium, or maximum, and how that would determine in what prison they would be serving their sentences. Frequently, I gave them some advice on how they could best make an adjustment to prison while serving those sentences. For some time after our car had been stolen, I had more questions for some of the prisoners.

I treated the armed robbers, drug offenders, and sex offenders with the usual routine objectivity, but if a car thief was unfortunate enough to have me as his interviewer, I would glare at him, narrowing my eyes, and snarl, "What makes you think that you can steal someone's car?" "Do you often take things which don't belong to you?" Or "Have you learned your lesson?"

It was hard to be sympathetic to thieves at the time I'd been victimized by one. I wanted our judicial system's long arm to reach out to that person and slap him with the maximum penalty. Remembering an incident in my senior year of high school helped temper my irritation.

I had dated my boyfriend, Clay, long enough to call it "serious." I wore his class ring, and we picked French fries from each other's plates. He trusted me with his most valued possession—his modified, hot, '54 Ford, and he clipped my earrings on the visor. Sometimes my girlfriends and I would sit in the Ford at lunch while it was parked in the school parking lot. One time an accidental spill of some pink nail polish on the dashboard sorely tested his love.

Clay had worked hard on making his car special, painting it a distinctive, sophisticated, shiny midnight blue and "souping" it up with pipes that made a sound I can only describe as a melodious jake brake with more trembling bass. The car had a presence all its own—a personality cars seldom have now.

When Clay went to college, his father, who owned the car, gave it to the next in-line brother, Willie. Our town was small, and we all knew who was there on Sunday evening after church because we rode down Main Street to see who else was cruising the streets in their distinctive cars. We knew Randy Vanda's turquoise and white '57 and Lawrence Merk's creamy yellow Impala. One Sunday night quite a few girls piled into my dad's Rambler—a really uncool car but better than the Hudson he had once owned. I drove down Main and took a side street to a church where, when kids paired off, they often parked a car before getting in with someone else. In the lot I saw the familiar blue '54 Ford.

"Hey," I said to the girls. "I have a key to that car." "Really?" more than one squealed. That's all it took. We piled in the car, too many of us for it, and I stepped on the clutch, started it, and shifted into first gear. The car came alive in my hands. We were having a great time talking and laughing while cruising at the twenty-five miles per hour speed limit and had made a few turns around Main Street. Then Ken Koop's black and white Chevy met us on the street.

Ken Koop and his girlfriend often double dated with Willie and his girl, and I could already see Willy in the backseat of the car—and animated movement. Then from behind the steering wheel of the Ford I saw Willie nearly shoot off the back seat toward the windshield. I heard Ken's horn blowing, but we slowed way down to take in the reaction. It's what we'd wanted all along. At that age, Willie had a slight, charming stutter that was exacerbated by seeing us in his Ford, and I could see him mouth the words, "Tha- that's my c-car." Our fun was short-lived. We let him know that the car was going back to the parking lot. Nothing we did after that would ever be as much fun as seeing Willie watch his car drive up the street.

The next day when I saw him at school, he did not look amused. He told me some tools his dad had in the back seat were now missing. My spirits sunk as quickly as though I'd fallen off a horse—my high horse. Shame took over. I thought about the lost tools, and how I could have had a car wreck and hurt people, and about Clay's folks. What would they think of me? I had not thought of what I did as anything more than a prank, but I had obviously done something far more serious. I could hardly concentrate on any of my classes the rest of the day, and by the time I got on the bus, I decided to tell Mom everything—hoping I would make it to her before someone else did. I dreaded telling her because even though Mom is good-natured, her parenting was basic. She was the type to defend the teachers if I was naughty without asking for my side of things. She was less about freedom of expression than shame and guilt and didn't smile about "sowing wild oats." She was not going to ask me, "So how do you feel about this?" It was enough that she would not feel good about it.

She was stirring something on the stove as I confessed everything to her. She may have sensed my deep embarrassment or appreciated my honesty, but we stood at the stove like adults confiding in each other. She spoke quietly, maybe so dad wouldn't hear us. She understood me while conveying to me that what I had done was serious. She named it. She said regardless of intentions, what I had done could be construed as car theft—not a joke, not a prank, not just fun.

When I think about it now, it seems hard to believe that it never crossed my mind that taking the Ford out for a spin was car theft. We didn't talk about joyriding or car theft or know people who stole cars.

A friend who has spent time in prison says when you're "on the streets" at an early age you don't think stealing is wrong. You think of it as survival, and you must "unlearn" stealing. Probably some of the young men sentenced to prison for car theft had reasons for stealing. Car theft may have had to do with survival—like getting to work on time or taking a family member to emergency—reasons far better than joyriding. Perhaps some of the young men didn't think at all. Perhaps they had no excuses except that they were young and impulsive. Maybe someone had even left the keys in a car, and it was easy to fall into crime, like falling in love. Maybe coming to prison was the difference between the engine starting and a dead battery.

We all ride on high horses, stopping short of falling off the cliff only because the horse stops, or we pull ourselves up short, or our parents take over the reins before the plunge. We hang on the precipice that keeps us from dropping the rest of the way.

Willie found the tools where they had slipped behind the back seat. My future in-laws never asked me to return the key. It wasn't necessary; I never used it again.

I can't say I stopped scowling at the young men sentenced to prison for car theft, but I tried to listen to their excuses and reasons for what they had done. I tried to be more understanding as I thought about Mom talking quietly to me about stealing, all the time stirring dinner and steering me in the right direction.

7

Sleeping in the Same Bed

. . . Those to whom evil is done
Do evil in return.

—W. H. AUDEN

"WE'VE LOST FOUR OF them already this year," Warden McKibben said frowning with disgust as he stepped into my office. Two female officers had been sexually involved with prisoners and fired for the felony. Earlier in the year a female teacher who had a relationship with one of her prison students who stayed later than the rest of the class was fired, and a few weeks later a naïve officer who claimed that she'd been raped, counting on other employees to believe that the prisoner was lying when he said it was mutual, was let go. Now we were down another two employees.

"I know," I said, almost apologetically. I felt defensive as though he blamed more women staff working in the prison than just those who were fired. As a deputy warden, I knew that many women had worked hard to do well in this predominantly male environment, and then a few lost their jobs because of one grave violation. I felt partly betrayed by them, and that judgment had somehow spread to include all of us. I worried that the dismissals would have a negative impact on hiring and promoting women.

The two women were shocked that they had been caught and charged, and fought for their jobs, undergoing lengthy investigations and then hiring lawyers in desperate attempts to keep their positions. Even when the evidence is convincing like being caught in the act, it was worth fighting. Corrections investigators could overlook something a good attorney is paid to find and possibly get them off the hook.

It's not that I didn't question how the women could throw away careers for a relationship with a prisoner. I always wondered about their circumstances and the reasons, but whys don't matter if there has been sex. There is either guilty or not. It's black and white.

Women were trained thoroughly about the hazards of the job and warned to watch for the signs making them vulnerable to manipulative prisoners. They were warned about involvement with prisoners, not only dangerous for them, but a felony. They knew some prisoners watched them 24/7, frequently observing them as carefully as their own families and learning about their susceptibilities. One of the officers, Sheila, had been going through a divorce. She'd gained weight. She came to work distracted and depressed, but Eddie who was doing seven years for armed robbery was there for her. They talked almost daily since Eddie was one of the porters who cleaned the hall under her supervision. He noticed her new hairstyle before anyone else did.

Prisoners eventually talk, even the one who's receiving favors. Prisons are secret places only to those who don't work or live there. Eddie wouldn't be able to resist bragging, and other prisoners alert to favors, are jealous of what someone like Eddie has going. Eddie told the investigator, "Look, I didn't intend to get her into trouble. I was surprised, man. I'm in here for seven, and this…she was great entertainment," he said with a grin.

The officers were already talking before the investigation and disciplinary conference were held. I detected the buzz in the unit that broke open the boredom like a fresh bleeding cut. I'd heard one officer say, "Geez, I was there for her. Why didn't she come to me instead of a co-o-o-onvict?" stretching out the first syllable.

Another articulated just what I'd worried about—that her dismissal would have a negative effect on the hiring and promotion of women—when he said, "This is no place for women," and I thought about what a former deputy warden had told me when I applied for a job at another prison a few years ago. "My wife is petite and blonde like you, and I wouldn't want her working here."

Officer Clark had reminded me of those dynamics. Some male officers thought that female officers were not strong enough to come to their rescue if prisoners assaulted them, or worse that female officers would become victims that needed rescuing. Officer Clark was a "fish," young with freckles, though he'd developed the swagger of some of the seasoned officers. He was just green enough to reveal things more experienced officers kept quiet, and let me know what the others were saying. "I went to Rick Stamine's cell in segregation last night. Haller was on too."

Maurine Haller was a little over five feet tall and confident. The male officers sometimes referred to her as the "social worker" a term officers used to describe others who they thought talked or listened to prisoners too much. Corrections Officers are trained to listen to prisoners and resolve conflicts, but when they finish their training and actually start working a prison unit, they encounter officers who encourage a healthy distance from the prisoners. They realize the necessity of finding a distinction between what they've learned and what is necessary to do in practice.

"I didn't think she'd be of much help when Stamine came out of his cell if he acted out, so I radioed for someone just in case."

"He's always cuffed behind his back, though, right?" I asked.

"Yeah, but he's too much for her."

I wanted to ask Officer Clark what Maurine Haller's strengths on the unit were. Women needed to be recognized and affirmed for what they achieve too. Male and female correctional officers have the same training and experience the same stress related to the job. Perhaps males are better at acting as a team. They slap each other on the back. They praise one another publicly whereas women, if they are complimented, receive compliments in private for things in which men excel. But there were few differences in their daily work.

I had seen Officer Maurine Haller interact with prisoners and their response to her seemed about the same as it was toward the male officers. Of course, all officers talked with prisoners and listened to them too. I'd heard the officers' conversations with prisoners on the unit. Some of the conversations that concerned me didn't end well for the prisoners.

Before meeting with the warden, I had walked down the hall and heard Officer Benning, an experienced officer, well-liked by the employees, in conversation with prisoners. His job that day was watching the prisoners sitting on the bench waiting for their medical appointments, a rather routine job.

"I must have lost your pass," he said to a prisoner named Jones, laughing. "Yeah, maybe I left it under your mother's bed."

"Oh, maaaan," the prisoner groaned, "You're too ugly for her," as he got back at Benning in their game of the "dozens."

Benning turned to Lenny, another prisoner who joked with him while on the bench. "On what horse did you ride in on?" The prisoners laughed. These young prisoners coming into the Reception Center didn't know the consequences of joking around with officers. They hadn't read the rules yet like the one that forbade "horse-play." Perhaps they thought that if it was an officer doing the teasing, it must be okay.

As I'd walked the halls making rounds in the unit, the prisoners asked to see me and complain about Benning. From his cell, Prisoner Lenny who had joked around with Benning asked to see me. "We were just playing around, joking, and all of a sudden Benning gets serious."

"What did you say to him?" I asked.

"That he must have the hots for Officer Curtis Miller, and he gets all mad and writes me an "insolence" ticket."

"Isn't Officer Miller a male? Surely you understand how inappropriate that is. You got yourself noticed," I said. "I can't help you. I wasn't there, and you have no witnesses."

"But that isn't fair." He almost wailed as he realized that other prisoners weren't the only complication in this place. I saw it dawning on him that the rules were for him, and he seethed, closing his mouth in a tight, resigned line, angry that he was such a sucker. It wasn't long before his anger found its way onto the unit.

Anyone who came to unlock Prisoner Lenny's cell so he could take his shower was in the way now. There was no excuse for Lenny's serious assault on an officer. It wasn't Officer Benning who took the bruising. Any officer walking the hall, unlocking doors, swinging keys, on his way home after his shift, maybe cocky, or whistling could have been a victim, a fist in his face. Lenny threw the punch at the officer's face.

The ticket which reported the assault was written and the report heard. It had the right time and date on it and was written with all the correct facts of the incident: what prisoner had been responsible for the assault, where it had happened in the unit, and how it had happened— down to the hand the prisoner had used on which cheek of the officer. The hearing about the ticket was held by the attorney, and Lenny was found guilty. Officers soon learned that if they wanted tickets on prisoners to "stick" with the attorneys, they needed to write them precisely. The tickets often used the same format when reporting the offense with names, dates, and times the only variations. I compared some tickets once, and asked an officer if what was on the misconduct ticket had perhaps happened somewhat differently. The officer not only denied it, but asked me if I didn't want her to write misconduct tickets for prisoner violations? Of course, employees must write tickets for violations. But for some staff writing misconduct tickets takes the place of managing and interacting with prisoners and resolving conflicts.

No one traced the line from the beginning of the story to Lenny's assault on the officer. Even if they had, what would it matter? The assault is what became important—significant to Prisoner Lenny who fell into Benning's trap. A psychologist recommended Lenny for impulse control therapy because of his anger after he spent some time in segregation.

Some employees are not fired when they become involved with prisoners. Involvement is not clear, not black and white as it was for the females dismissed for sexual involvement with prisoners, but as gray as an officer's uniform. Maybe someone is bored or has a bad day. One remark or action leads to another, escalating until an officer thinks the teasing or playing the dozens has gone too far, and writes a misconduct ticket. But the prisoner does not have power. He's always the one found guilty. The prisoner's misconduct raises his security level. He is transferred to another prison, goes to segregation, or learns to look straight ahead doing his own time, maybe waits for an officer to listen to him like Eddie listening to Sheila. Employees, like the female officers fired and Benning who stays employed, are cut from the same cloth as the prisoners. Inappropriately, some even lie with them in the same bed.

8

Not Always as It Seems

ONE DAY MY SISTER Ruth, intending to cut up some meat she'd taken from the refrigerator, took out a large butcher knife. When she heard her dog, Bear, yelping in the yard, she dropped the knife. She opened the back door to find her gentle black dog bleeding profusely. Another dog had attacked and wounded Bear in her own yard. Ruth left the knife and Bear's blood on the kitchen floor and rushed Bear to the vet where the dog received medicine and stitches that eventually led to her recovery. Meanwhile my brother-in-law, Jim, came home, found a bloody kitchen and a large knife, and drew his own conclusions. I tease Ruth. "Next time someone's going to stab and abduct you, please leave a note."

Things are not always as they seem on the surface. For those of us working with prisoners, sometimes our gut tells us if a prisoner is particularly dangerous, but that doesn't happen most of the time. Prisoners are not villains or good guys. They don't hiss like Hannibal Lector in the 1991 movie *Silence of the Lambs* or become heroes like Tim Robbins in *Shawshank Redemption* (1994). In fact, some of those prisoners who behave badly and call attention to themselves are not the most dangerous prisoners, while others, maybe outwardly quiet and orderly, are harboring rage and primed to explode.

When I worked in a women's prison, I spoke frequently with an articulate and intelligent inmate. She wanted a college degree. I thought she had surely committed a white collar crime: embezzlement, or fraud. When I read her file, I found she had stabbed someone in a pick-up truck. Not a cleverly devised scheme requiring knowledge in the area of finance or banking, but a messy, bloody crime. I didn't recognize the person from her record. Her prison facade and the description of how she behaved when she committed her crime were strikingly different. Like anyone, prisoners also often hide behind a veneer of respectability.

In another prison, I observed a well-mannered prisoner clerk working in the school office. He was polite, quiet, and efficient. His demeanor was calm and cool. Employees asked him questions about office procedures, and he answered my questions several times before I looked at his prisoner file. In a rage, he had slaughtered his family. Like other employees, I was often surprised by the backgrounds of quiet, well-behaved prisoners.

In 1984 Jennifer Thompson was a bright college student with a promising future. One evening a man broke into her apartment and raped her. He stayed for half an hour. What is unusual is that Jennifer desperately tried to pay attention so this wouldn't happen to others. She tried to memorize details and features of his face. The police got a composite sketch based on her description. An anonymous tip identified the perpetrator, Ronald Cotton, who already had a conviction on his record and had served time. Objects like a red flashlight found in his apartment had been used in the rape. His alibi didn't check out. He was arrested. Jennifer was shown six photos and identified Cotton. *She was not told that she didn't need to choose any of the photos if the person who attacked her was not shown on any of the photos.* Instead she was told she did a good job of identification.

Such horrendous crimes call for conviction. She identified Cotton in a line-up though he denied he was guilty. Rumors surfaced in prison that Bobbie Poole was the man who had raped Jennifer, and indeed he was, but she denied that he was. After serving fourteen years, Cotton was exonerated by DNA evidence. Until a distinction was made, a man paid with part of his life—the wrong man.[1]

Philip Markoff made headlines when he robbed two women, and in April 2009 he killed Julissa Brisman in a hotel. Markoff had been seen as a clean cut former medical student, and was engaged to be married, but he had a dark secret. Through ads placed on Craigslist, he met women who became his victims. He became known as the "Craigslist Killer." Markoff committed suicide while awaiting trial after his indictment for first-degree murder, armed robbery, and other charges.[2]

1. Doyle, "Eyewitness Memory," Lecture.
2. Ford, "Alleged Craiglist Killer Philip Markoff Found Dead in Jail," 2010.

Sometimes the daily routines of the prison seem almost comfortable, and employees can become complacent. Everyone is in his or her place. The sun shines, flowers grow, and birds sing. Prisoners settle in, and walk to meals, school, and work in an orderly and ordinary way most of the time. Prisons may appear to be controlled, orderly places even though they house violent offenders. A sense of complacency can fool prison staff and cost lives.

During my career I've spoken to people whose response to a gut feeling has helped us avert an emergency in the prison. These employees investigated their hunches and found out their suspicions were based on prisoners' real plots that could have led to an escape or injury to staff. Sometimes lives are saved by instincts and hunches that come into play when one is trying to survive, and we learn something new.

Several years ago my husband and I, along with one other hiker, took a boat through Gates of the Mountains near Helena, Montana to a remote area, Mann Gulch, where on August 5, 1949 sixteen smokejumpers lost their lives in a forest fire. Only two of them and the foreman, Wag Dodge survived. Their story, in *Young Men and Fire* (1992) written by Norman Maclean, remains one of my favorite books. Maclean writes the book like an investigation about what occurred and honors the men who died that day. These young men were not supposed to die. They were the Green Berets of smokejumpers, and the fire looked manageable at first until it suddenly began burning below them at the mouth of the gulch. As a result of the tragedy, we know more about fire science, and the winds and conditions that can cause fire explosions.

We disembarked from the boat on a warm summer day, watching for rattlesnakes in the dry grass. As my husband and I walked on the slopes of Mann Gulch, we occasionally saw a piece of charred wood from the fire. Mann Gulch is no vacation destination and tourists have not scoured the area for souvenirs. The tools the men dropped were removed not that long ago. At a higher level we touched the granite crosses placed where each man is believed to have fallen to the fire. The slope is very steep. I hike and and I jog four miles three times weekly, but even with the motivation of a fire raging behind me I could hardly imagine that two of the men outran the fire and climbed ahead to safety by going through the cleft of a rock near the ridge to the other side. Wag Dodge, the foreman also survived and became the subject of a controversy and investigation that raged like the fire.

When Wag Dodge saw that his crew could not outrun the fire, he did something that mystified the men. He lit an escape fire, setting matches to an area of the grass which burned, and told the men to lie down in the burned area. His command was so counterintuitive to everything the men knew that some of them cursed him and kept running. Dodge lay in the burned out area while the raging fire blew over him. Some of the victims' family members accused Dodge of setting a fire that killed members of his crew. When Dodge was asked how he knew to light that fire, he said he didn't know. If only the men had lain on the ground in Dodge's burned out area. Instinctual, gut feelings caused some to run, and instinct caused Dodge to build a fire. In prison I learned from employees who knew that life is not always the way it seems and who trusted their instincts.

Malcolm Gladwell in "The Naked Face" writes about people who have highly developed instincts or training that enable them to make good snap judgments about people. Some of the judgments people make with these shrewd skills seem to defy common sense. They read faces for all the voluntary as well as involuntary expressions. Gladwell reports that John Yarbrough was working night patrol one evening for the Los Angeles County Sheriff's Department when a man only a few yards away pointed a gun at him. Yarbrough had a gun, but did not shoot the man. Yarbrough admits it was a dangerous situation, but logic had nothing to do with his decision. He had a gut reaction that told him the man was not an imminent threat, and when Yarbrough asked him to, the man backed down. Most of us can't predict which prisoners will commit crimes either in prison or once they are released, and would appreciate a skill like Yarbrough's.

Emergencies in prison often require sudden decisions and immediate action. We've learned to survive by evaluating people (and prisoners) quickly, and we're often right. But I don't have that intuitive skill Yarbrough had. I may have drawn the same conclusion my brother-in-law did when he saw the knife in a bloody kitchen. Too often I have judged people with whom I work on first impressions and was wrong. I did not expect to learn so much from people whose skills were different from mine. I'm still amazed how widely dissimilar people complement each other in the Corrections environment. It seems a microcosm of what community should be.

9

Fine Distinctions

WHEN THE CAPTAIN BROUGHT Lieutenant Jeffries to my office for introductions, the new Lieutenant shook my hand and called me Ma'am instead of "Deputy." It was the "I'll respect you because of your position" or "I have had good discipline and training," perhaps in the military, I couldn't tell which. Our handshaking did not connect us. "How do you feel about working with mentally-ill prisoners?" I asked.

Lieutenant Jeffries is not someone I would have selected for the job. I had interviewed many candidates, but I did not make the hiring decisions alone. All the ratings of the interview team went into the final decision. Jeffries had answered the questions quite well. The part in his hair was straight, his uniform pressed and fitting, and he looked strong, the kind of spit-and-polish guy a mother might like her daughter to date. It was the standing at attention, with chest expanded as though he had taken a breath and wouldn't let go, that bothered me. He reminded me of a cat, hair bristling, walking sideways to look more imposing to an enemy.

Meeting him reminded me of my short experience with water at the local health club. When I took swimming lessons and tried to remember the arm and leg strokes, while turning my face to breathe—the steps that would come automatically to a child—I'd forget to breathe as though once inflated lungs would keep me afloat forever. Perhaps the new lieutenant, like me, had so much on his mind he'd forgotten to breathe.

"It's a new challenge," he said, not about to let a casual remark get him into trouble. I asked him more questions, and he was courteous, humorless, his eyes steady. I didn't think I'd know what he felt or thought. He would say what was necessary, what he thought I'd like to hear. He would call me when policy required it, and we wouldn't mull over things much. He wouldn't need much advice. Not even several beers in a bar would loosen him up. He had done well as an officer and remained on guard.

The prison is a place of control. As employees, we control our schedules, how we look and behave, and our activities during our working time in the prison. The control is part of the discipline of working in a paramilitary organization, designed to keep everyone safe, and show the prisoners that we are in charge. A prison's hub of communication, security, and control is fittingly called the Control Center. For all the state-of-the-art equipment, we know that the prisoners outnumber us, and that none of us has complete control. Critical incidents, like assaults, theft, and escapes occur, though infrequently in this atmosphere drenched in control.

However, the prisoners themselves have very little control over the daily activities of their lives within prisons. We tell them when to get up, how and when to make their beds, when and what to eat, and what they will be doing if they have prison jobs or participate in school or counseling programs. We require them to follow many rules, and if they break those rules consequences swiftly follow in the form of misconduct tickets. With these conditions, it's not surprising that prisoners exercise whatever control they have.

Lieutenant Jeffries hadn't worked long as a lieutenant when he called me at home on the weekend. I was the deputy on duty and would be called in the event of emergencies, but if something happened, the prison would be an hour into the crisis by the time I arrived. I'm sure some employees welcomed a crisis to test their mettle or to relieve the monotony. I thrived on the routine that prisons are most of the time.

"Deputy, something has just happened I've never experienced in my years with Corrections." His voice told me something was wrong. Our careers spread out before us. I expected the worst and hoped I'd know what to do about the problem. We had one escape this year though the prisoner had been caught. We'd also had a hostage incident recently. My heart was racing.

Go on, spit it out, I wanted to say.

He blurted it out. "A prisoner in segregation has smeared feces all over his cell."

"Whaa, what?" I wanted to laugh. I was relieved. No escape, hostage taking, or suicide—and relief I was not there. Not anywhere at prison or on that prisoner's housing unit where other prisoners would be vocal and putting up a stink about the stink. Not a critical incident, although a simple, crazy, frustrating "shit happens" day. This type of incident unnerves all of us.

I gave Lieutenant Jeffries the best advice I had. I let him know employees knew what to do under these unpleasant circumstances. The air seemed to come out of his chest now that he was calling for help. He had cracked open and was like the rest of us, delightfully vulnerable and seeking. I had underestimated him.

The psychologists didn't work on the weekend and wouldn't be available. The employees had the prison workers clean up the cell, and then moved the prisoner to another cell. Lieutenant Jeffries and I talked about things—about how crazy prisoners could be, how frustrating, afraid, and inappropriate—like all of us. I knew he had been rational and calm with his staff and the prisoners, and that he didn't care who gave him advice just as long as it resulted in getting done what had to be done.

The next morning I made rounds in the unit of the incident and asked if a psychologist had seen the prisoner. One of the segregation officers said, "Not yet, but he probably doesn't need to see one."

"Why?" I asked.

"He isn't mentally ill," said the officer.

"Oh?" I asked wondering about how the officer had arrived at that judgment.

"Well," he said, "the prisoner had just smeared the poop, not eaten it."

Right, I thought. A mere smear. If he had eaten it, he would be mentally ill. Of course. Right out of the textbook of working daily with mentally ill prisoners. Those of us who are working directly with prisoners make fine distinctions too, imitating the psychologists, drawing lines between who is mentally ill and, who is not, deciding who will be seen and how they will be housed.

10

The Lieutenant and Tony

"Unless the Lord watches over the city,
the watchmen stand guard in vain."

—PSALM 127:1

DEPUTY WARDENS WORKED MORE evenings after September 11, 2001, but I had not planned to stay late the night Prisoner Tony Kuzan confronted Lietenant Cariek. The prison population was large at this prison, but I knew who Kuzan was, and from my office window overlooking the yard I could see him hanging around the basketball court. It was close to 1600 hours, and the shadows of the arms and legs crisscrossed on the court making the prisoners look tall and lanky in the fast setting sun.

I was sure Lieutenant Cariek could also see Kuzan from the window in the prison's Control Center where I knew the Lieutenant would be busy with all the communications, prisoner movement, security equipment and paperwork that kept supervisors enclosed there. I didn't wait for him to come to my office to talk about an officer or one of the prisoners as he often did. If he had a few minutes before he made his rounds in the prison, I'd discuss the new procedure for mentally ill prisoners with him while he was in the Control Center, a short walk from my office. I walked in the Control Center with a copy of the new procedure.

"Hello Lieutenant," I said as he finished writing a routine note in the logbook. "When you have a minute, could I talk with you about OP-FCF 31.01?" He looked up from the logbook with a quizzical look. At this time of the day, deputy wardens would only be asking him to do more than he was already doing on second shift.

"Now is okay," he said grinning but with one eyebrow raised. The procedure was long and cumbersome, and remembering its many steps would not come naturally when confronted with some of the behaviors of our mentally ill prisoners. Sometimes there's little time to remember what is written in the procedures when prisoners lash out, perhaps assaulting someone, and quick action is necessary. What we do by instinct to protect those who are victims is not always the same as what's written in the procedures. I was relieved when employees responded quickly to a crisis and did it right almost automatically because they knew it so well. Others depended on the orders of their supervisors. Being reflective and referring to policy or procedure was a luxury under such circumstances.

Lieutenant Cariek was close to retirement. He had not been with Corrections his whole career. The talk was that he had not worked out so well with the State Police. But he was not an employee we were "forced" to take. He wasn't what employees disparagingly called just a "warm body." He had the background, physique, and training that many Corrections' supervisors found desirable, and he followed orders—reasons that likely led to his promotions.

When he made rounds, it was less to evaluate those he supervised and more to "kick it" with them. I wished he were more thoughtful, but his experience was solid. He related to both prisoners and employees, and I heard few complaints about him. He looked through the window to the prisoner yard.

"Did you see Kuzan out there?" he asked. It was getting dark, and most of the prisoners were moseying back to their housing units in anticipation for the announcement to take count—all except Tony Kuzan who lingered behind talking trash with another prisoner near the basketball court. Once count was announced on the speaker, the prisoner talking with Tony left for his cell. "I'm keeping an eye on him. Officers report that he's resisting following the housing rules."

We watched Tony laughing and calling out to the prisoner he was talking to, and I hoped he'd return to his housing unit for count. Lt. Cariek and I turned to the procedure. I showed him the twenty pages that all employees would be required to read and sign. He looked at the document and ran his hand over his sandy colored short hair. He frowned as though this were an obstacle to overcome. "Central Office was busy thinking this one up."

Employees often talked about Central Office as though it existed to make more work for us or was a separate entity unfamiliar with the workings of the prison. I had not worked in Central Office long, but I understood why folks who didn't know the individuals working there might be cynical. "Well," I reminded him, defending the procedure, "typically people who work in the prisons are on the committees when operating procedures are written. If we just look at how the steps have changed in the new version and are different from how we've been doing things, and then review the rest, it will go faster. Then let me know if you think we'll be able to implement it."

"What choice do we have?" Cariek grinned. He didn't ask any questions I could perhaps answer about policy. He knew the routines and the prisoners better than he knew the written rules. I had a feeling he wouldn't teach the employees too much about the fine distinctions in the new procedure and that he'd treat Tony and the mentally ill prisoners like the rest of the prisoners, assuming that everyone who came to prison had problems.

One of the psychologists had "screened" Tony, but it was not necessary to separate him from what we called the general population prisoners. The criteria for who would be designated mentally ill were tight. Few beds were available, and they were reserved for the most severe depending on who was most in need or most likely to harm someone. Mental health professionals sometimes left written instructions in logbooks for how particular prisoners should be treated in housing, or they contacted us verbally if a prisoner was to be watched or treated somewhat differently than general population prisoners.

However, many prisoners were vulnerable and "restricted" in special cells so they would not mix with other inmates. Maybe, so the reasoning went, if he were restricted like this other prisoners would not prey upon Tony or take what he bought from the store or bribe him. To me he seemed vulnerable like a patient on an operating table ready for surgery, though other prisoners, desperate for what they could get, were often better at detecting those who seemed susceptible to manipulation. Tony's larger size and his impulsiveness would both help him survive and get him in trouble.

Most of the other employees didn't know which terms the psychologists had used to describe Tony in his file. Was he socially inadequate? Did he suffer from mental illness or from what was still called retardation? With the number of prisoners to manage, we had little time for making distinctions. I knew Tony as much as I knew many prisoners that approached me when I made rounds. He was usually slack-jawed and grinning. In spite of his size he had not adopted the mask that many prisoners donned that said, leave me alone, I'm tough. But tonight his jaw was set, and his eyes blazed. As though a flag had been waved, he seemed about to stampede.

Instead of heading for his unit, he walked in the opposite direction toward the Control Center where we stood. Prisoners were not allowed near the Control Center especially at count time unless they had written passes or were transferring to other prisons or going on parole, none of which was the case with Tony. Lt. Cariek stepped out of the Control Center to meet him. Tony looked wild and determined. I had been on my way to my office but instead waited where I could see Tony but he couldn't see me.

"Where are you going?" the Lieutenant Cariek asked.

"I'm going to Cuba." I heard Tony say.

"Where is your pass?" asked the lieutenant.

"God is my pass." Tony said defiantly, as though he knew Him.

Prisoners had expectations of justice and ways of reminding us that we all respond to a higher authority. Who can argue with that? I resisted laughing about that spiritual "pass."

But he followed it with, "I can get violent."

I sensed that he was parroting something he'd heard or saw recorded in his file. Still, there was a problem. He had already violated the rules.

Wasting no time, the lieutenant said, "No, you won't."

Still belligerent, Tony shot back, "Why not?"

"Because if you get violent, I'll knock you right through that wall."

I cringed. Employees were often calm and acted objectively when prisoners were hostile, defusing their angry outbursts. I was sure the Lieutenant's "threat" would escalate Tony's anger prompting a bigger row. The seconds seemed to stretch into minutes.

Suddenly Tony's face brightened, and he smiled. "Oh, okay then." Cariek smiled too, and they both laughed.

"Now get back to your housing unit." Tony turned and ran across the yard to his housing unit.

No bigger conflict occurred escalating the altercation. No calls for backup or help. Perhaps Tony had longed for some structure or contact with an employee, and the Lieutenant had detected the simple desire behind Tony's words. Or Lieutenant Cariek had realized that Tony wished to try out some new bluster he had acquired on the yard when other prisoners were not around, and where he would not need to "save face." Perhaps the Lieutenant didn't want to write a threatening behavior ticket, wait for it to be reviewed, or place Tony in segregation, pending the outcome of the verdict. Tony may have diffused the incident with a smile or the Lieutenant with a laugh. More likely, the Lieutenant behaved toward the prisoner as though he were an equal, and Tony realized that if he didn't treat people with respect they would not show him respect either. After all, this is the way it is on the streets.

That night Tony went where he didn't always go—man to man instead of prisoner to authority—and where both behaved differently as though the Lieutenant didn't always say what was expected, and Tony didn't always have to be crazy.

No employee has a monopoly on responding well to prisoners—not those who deliberate, act quickly, or those with the most education. Sometimes in spite of our idiosyncrasies, prisoners understand. Who knows them best? Those in authority? Professionals? Those meeting with them when there is a crisis? Or officers, sergeants, lieutenants, and captains working daily with them where they live?

I often think about Tony, boldly coming to the Control Center, the place of the center of communications, security, and authority—the holy of holies in the prison—and arriving there at count time in a place where we are trained to believe we have control and authority.

Tony would not be seen as crazy for being violent or disobeying a rule. But mentioning "God" without so much as a "damn" behind it, as though he was familiar with Him, that was a sign of craziness. All he may have been after was to be counted, not the way we take count to make sure he was there, but to be more than a number and remind us there are higher authorities than Corrections employees, and that his God made rounds to see prisoners, the mentally ill, or those called crazy.

Lt. Cariek had experience working with prisoners and Tony went back to his housing unit without a fight. I represented the twenty pages of procedure. I was like the kid who is home for vacation after one year of college, and as my parents said, knows everything. I was the kid coming home with a head full of sociology and psychology only to realize too late, as she waits in a ditch to be rescued that it takes a different kind of smarts than sociology to drive on a snow-covered road.

And yet twenty pages of procedure should not be scuttled. While we respect those in authority and those who write procedures, we shouldn't be surprised when something that sounds like the truth comes from the lowly, poor, prisoners and others on the margins who don't promote us. Sometimes knowledge and experience are on the table, but we travel in other territory where words spoken resonate like wisdom and remind us we do not have the last word.

11

Making Distinctions: An Investigation

RECORDING EMPLOYEES' CONVERSATIONS WAS against the rules, and yet a Resident Unit Manager (RUM) had brought in the recorder and claimed he had taped a psychiatrist making racist comments. Specifically, he claimed the psychiatrist had come into the housing unit to see a prisoner and had asked, *"What's the name of that lame useless nigger?"* and that it was recorded on tape.

I wasn't investigating the violation of bringing in the tape recorder. That investigation was assigned later to someone else. I'd been assigned to investigate the recording on the tape.

I began preparing my questionnaires for the investigation of the few people to ask the who, what, when, where, and how of things. When the RUM allegedly recorded the psychiatrist, there were few witnesses, and they had not heard what was recorded on the tape. But rumors circulated, and what was supposedly on the tape had polarized the staff along racial lines. The RUM was black, and he'd brought the tape to the head nurse who was also black, and she gave it to the warden. Other black employees had already heard about the contents on the tape though they had not listened to it, and were upset, assuming the worst. The psychiatrist was white, and angry about the tape, about answering questions, and about the investigation.

Because answering those questions feels so much like accusation, employees often must be told they are not guilty unless the evidence shows it. The deputy warden or warden reads the investigation, and the person who committed the alleged violation is either charged with the violation or not charged. If charged, the one accused is entitled to a disciplinary conference.

Officers' actions are investigated most frequently. They form the majority of employees, and because of their direct contact with prisoners they are more likely to be accused of violating the rules. Healthcare personnel, administrators, and supervisors are often more upset when investigated because they provide services for prisoners at a different level and pride themselves on being educated professionals and being above making errors or violating rules. The psychiatrist ran into me by the time clock and snarled at me.

"This is ridiculous. I don't know why I work here. This is bullshit." I wanted to tell him he was not guilty unless charged, but I didn't. I knew how he felt.

As an administrator, I've often been surprised at what I've found in investigations of incidents. I have sent investigations back to investigators because I didn't think the evidence was strong enough to charge an employee. I've read some I thought would never stick, certain the person would file a grievance, and the matter would go to arbitration where it would not be supported. Then I would be surprised when it was upheld.

Others looked so sound on paper. Evidence *ad infinitum* had been collected, and not a detail seemed to be missing, but the person was not charged, or no one had considered a technicality, or an employee's good past record would be considered, and the accused would receive minor sanctions or not be charged at all.

Good investigations take time, but they are challenging. I tried to anticipate the arguments the persons who had "allegedly" violated a rule would make to defend themselves. Sometimes I imagined the people who were being investigated were set up and being retaliated against for something they had done, and might be found guilty when they were not.

Police investigations of crimes have increasingly come under scrutiny, and a focus on investigative procedures has improved them in part because of DNA. Of course, there is often not DNA. A drive-by shooting leaves no blood, semen, or hairs for examination. But DNA has such a dramatic impact on solving crimes that it influences investigators to examine all evidence more cautiously, introducing scientific inquiry and objectivity into a process where oversight is sorely needed.

The witness should know that one of the choices in a line-up is "none of them." In 2006, victims of the alleged Duke University rape case, when asked to identify offenders, were shown pictures only of the lacrosse players, leaving them with the impression that they were shown the only possible offenders.[1]

Victims and witnesses overlook differences in people not of their race. Introducing conversations and details or newspaper articles may become part of what the witness thinks they remember. We now know that every exchange and conversation, and the way questions are asked, is an opportunity for contamination of the evidence.

In Virginia a woman who worried about the sniper attacks by John Allen Muhammad did not report a suspicious blue car because police were looking for a white van. A police officer spoke to Muhammad but let him go because he was in the blue car.[2] Though they may have every intention of being reliable, eye witnesses are not always accurate. Our hearing is also not always reliable. Just as people who see the same accident report it differently, what they hear is often different. One witness may report the screech of tires and another, the sound of glass shattering. Recordings may have flaws subjecting them to interpretation.

I was not in law enforcement and fortunately the investigation I was assigned was not an investigation of a rape or homicide. Although violations of Corrections' employees vary in their severity the incidents investigated by Corrections' employees are rule violations rather than criminal offenses which are investigated by the state police. But the answers at the end are "guilty" or "not guilty," and small distinctions matter. Several years ago wardens were frustrated about the large number of investigations and disciplinary conferences at the prisons and frustrated because investigations are time-consuming, generate paperwork, and the disciplinary conferences that follow can be tedious.

At a wardens' meeting someone proposed that perhaps not all those investigated need go through a disciplinary process. Perhaps a good ol' ass chewing was enough. I began to wonder. What would the parameters of an "ass chewing" be? What was okay and not okay? What could and could not be said? How would we determine a "good" from a "bad" review? Would some people come under the disciplinary process, and others have the ass chewing? Could one choose what to have if charged with a violation? Would someone with a smooth tongue fare better than someone nervous and unpopular? Would violators prefer it to the cumbersome disciplinary process? What distinctions should be made?

1. Bissinger, "Duke's Laccrosse Scandal," 72.

2. Barisic, "Sniper Trial Highlights Missed Opportunities to End Spree," Associated Press, 2003.

The discussion of ass chewing made what we have for rules and the disciplinary process, regardless of how flawed, look good. Investigations and disciplinary conferences are desirable. There are rarely shortcuts to justice. The outcome of the investigation I was assigned showed the importance of careful analysis.

I listened to the tape on a tape recorder—first at normal speed and then slowly. The psychiatrist certainly could have said what was alleged. He could have said, *"that lame useless nigger,"* but the words were not clear. Finally, upon the warden's recommendation, I took the tape to the Michigan State Police lab where it could be played on more sophisticated equipment and analyzed. The police at the lab did not know what was on the tape. We did not tell them about the allegation.

The police officer took me to a rather dark room full of wires and taping equipment as though good lighting might distract the sounds on the tape. He inserted the tape, and played it back slowly. It was clear. I could hear the voice and words of the psychiatrist as though he were talking in the room. The officer asked me what I'd heard. I repeated what the psychiatrist had said, *"The inmate retains his youthful vigor."* The officer in the lab agreed.

Just as lawsuits don't always make things right, investigations do not always solve conflicts. This one left a residue of bitterness. The psychiatrist remained irritated. Some of the employees were skeptical, others quiet, and still others puzzled. Racism at the prison didn't go away even though the psychiatrist had not used a racial slur in this incident or investigation.

Investigations may not be ideal and disciplinary conferences time-consuming, but they are about the best way of finding out the facts—and the truth, as elusive as that can be. This was one small investigation in one prison and two phrases sounding alike yet as different as guilty and not guilty. Because a warden suggested that the Michigan Police lab play the tapes, and it was investigated, we avoided charging a psychiatrist with making a racist comment. Imagine how much more could have been on the line.

This particular investigation's solution raises a larger problem. Hearing something through another medium like the telephone or a recording may distort what was said. But to what extent does the stress of working in an environment where there is talk of racism contribute to mishearing what is spoken? Perhaps racist comments made at other times and in different situations influenced what the Resident Unit Manager "heard." Perhaps the Resident Unit Manager left the tape recorder on and waited for the psychiatrist to talk and use a racist slur, certain that the recorder would be objective. Those who are the subjects of investigations expect fairness, but we know investigators and witnesses approach each incident with human bias. We judge, interpret, and draw conclusions on the evidence screened through our biases, and piece together stories from the words we think we hear and the sights we think we see. A recent trial reported in the May 3, 2010 *New Yorker* illustrates how we weave narratives from the facts.

According to Janet Malcolm, a word or phrase on tape, interpreted differently with considerably different results, was part of a murder trial in New York in 2009. A female doctor named Mazoltuv Borukhova was on trial for allegedly hiring an assassin named Mallayev, who was also on trial, to kill Mazoltuv's husband, Daniel Malakov, also a doctor.

In the fourth week of the trial, an audiotape was found in Borukhova's apartment recording a conversation between Borukhova and Mallayev, speaking in Bukhori and Russian. The conversation, recorded by Borukhova in her car, took place five months before the murder and was initially considered mundane and unrelated to the murder. The recording of the dialogue was described as "garbled" and "fragmentary" and a stunning case of the "malleability of trial evidence." In the final lines which surprised the courtroom, Mallayev seemed to say to Borukhova, "Are you going to make me happy?" to which she replied, "Yes." Whether she was sleeping with Mallayev or talking about paying him to murder her husband were equally bad for Borukhova's case until she translated what he had said. She claimed Mallayev had used the word, *padayesh* meaning, "Are you getting out of the car?" and not *obraduesh*, "Are you going to make me happy?"

Malcolm goes on to say that the mishearing favored the prosecution and "advanced their narrative," almost by design, unconsciously, and then adds this: "We go through life mishearing and misseeing (sic) and misunderstanding so that the stories we tell ourselves will add up."[3] Our brains work to make disparate pieces of a puzzle fit.

3. Malcolm, "Iphigenia in Forest Hills," 37–38.

12

Women Prisoners Breaking the Silence

Said I Wasn't Gonna Tell Nobody
But I Couldn't Keep It to Myself.

—ABYSSINIAN BAPTIST CHOIR, SONY MUSIC DISTRIBUTION, 1994.
LYRICS, PROFESSOR ALEX BRADFORD

"Because incest and domestic violence cut across the economic divide,
women of all means are schooled in silence."

—WALLY LAMB[1]

FLORENCE CRANE CORRECTIONAL FACILITY in Coldwater was one of only two correctional facilities for women in Michigan when I took a position there as Assistant Deputy Warden in the late '80s. At the time I didn't expect that working with female prisoners would be much different than working with male prisoners. It is, and in ways difficult to define. Like grammar, there are exceptions to the "rules." For example, females are generally more verbal than male prisoners though some male prisoners are talkative. Many female prisoners have been abused prior to their incarceration. Of course, many male prisoners were abused and victims of violence too, but the pattern of victimization is more pronounced for females. In addition, the shame women feel about abuse in families or acquaintances keeps victims silent until the effects of abuse fester and become a factor leading to crimes.

1. Lamb, "Couldn't Keep It To Ourselves," 9.

According to Wally Lamb in the book *I'll Fly Away*, 70 percent of incarcerated women have been the victims of incest and sexual violence. Kelley Blanchette and Kelly N. Taylor report that the "typical" female trajectory in the criminal justice system begins with an abusive home environment followed by leaving home and living on the streets, further victimization, and substance abuse. Prostitution, fraud, and theft are the common crimes leading to imprisonment. [2]

In the book *Couldn't Keep it to Myself*, edited by Wally Lamb, women in the York Correctional Institution for Women in Connecticut break their silence to tell stories of traumatic abuse. One of the women was serving time for murdering her husband, filed divorce papers while he was with another woman for two weeks, tries to pull the papers back when he comes home so loving. But she's too late. The papers had been filed. Furious, he tells her she can't have anyone else in her life. It's okay for him to have another lover, but not for her. "What's yours is mine, and what's mine is mine," he tells her.

The following weekend they drive to see her father some distance away. While he is driving, he tells her he must watch out for cops, he has a couple of guns in the car. She realizes she's told no one she is going on this trip or where she's going. After two hours, they take a mountain road in search of a trail. The road becomes narrow. "There's a cabin around here," he said. "Let's walk the rest of the way." He gets his gun. She asks him if he came all this way to shoot targets. He tells her, "No, I came all this way to show you how easy it would be to make you disappear." He plays "Killing Me Softly with His Song" for two hours on the way home. She realizes he doesn't want a divorce. He can make her disappear. [3]

The story and others are full of suspense, and after reading a few of them, I could almost predict the common elements leading to what happens in each one. The names and places and circumstances vary, but like a car out of control, each frank story tells of a woman careening down a slope into an often sickening conclusion. While reading, I wanted to say, "run", or "fly away" as the title suggests. Some of the women were physically and sexually abused by a father or stepfather they trusted before they knew what abuse or sex was. Many female prisoners were victimized, and then, desperate for attention, married an abusive partner or became addicted to drugs to medicate their pain. Some prisoners suffer

2. Blanchette and Taylor, "Reintegration of Female Offenders," 61.
3. Lane, "Puzzle Pieces," 229–30.

from post traumatic stress disorder at the time they arrive in prison. Blanchette and Taylor report that post-traumatic stress may also lead to behaviors that include the use of alcohol and other drugs.

Some of the women lashed out and murdered a boyfriend or husband because they felt trapped. A common theme of their histories is how hopeless they felt in their situations as though there were no exit. In the book, *I'll Fly Away,* one woman prisoner from the Connecticut prison in a Survivors of Abuse group finds it strange that all the females' menfolk, strangers to each other, used such similar phrases, phrases such as:

> I'm going to do whatever I want to do whenever I want to do it.
> No one else would ever want you, so you'd better get used to it.
> Sweetie, I'd die without you.
> I swear it's never going to happen again.
> Where could you go where I wouldn't find you? [4]

The stories are about the women incarcerated in Connecticut, but they could be about women anywhere.

Aileen Wuornos, born in Rochester, Michigan in 1956, and a serial killer, was convicted and executed in 2002 in Florida. The movie *Monster* (2003) is about part of her life, when in 1989, she claimed that while working as a prostitute she was severely beaten by a man. Before she was found and arrested, she killed him and another six men who picked her up after that.

Wuornos was severely abused as a child. Her mother was fifteen when she married Aileen's father, but divorced him before Wuornos was born. She never met her father who was in prison for the rape and attempted murder of an eight year-old boy. She was adopted by her grandparents and claimed that her grandfather sexually assaulted her. Pregnant at age fourteen, she began supporting herself as a prostitute. She hitchhiked to Florida and was arrested for passing forged checks, driving under the influence, auto theft, assaults, and other crimes before her string of murders.[5]

When I worked at Florence Crane, I didn't hear many of the prisoners' stories. After I left Florence Crane for another position, I began reading about sexual abuse in women's prisons. In the early '90s, one

---

4. Parsons, "Reawakening Through Nature: A Prison Reflection," 223.

5. Wikipedia, "Aileen Wuornos," 1–10.

hundred prisoners in a prison in Georgia brought a lawsuit against the state. Indictments uncovered a culture of sexual activity, harassment, and abuse. A newly appointed warden named Mary Espositio reported in *Fortune News*, February 1994, "If this isn't happening at other prisons, I'd be amazed."[6]

David Kaiser and Lovisa Stannow report in *The New York Review of Books*, "Prison Rape and the Government," March 24, 2011, that in 1998 Jan Lastocy, who was serving a sentence for embezzlement in a Michigan prison, worked in a warehouse near a men's prison. She was supervised by three corrections officers, and one of them raped her. She hoped to be released and be home with her husband and children in a few months so she kept quiet. During the next few months, the officer raped her repeatedly. She was terrified, and also felt guilty because the officer raped other women at the facility. She wrote a poem about the fears she had of getting tickets, having her time lengthened, and of not being believed or mattering to anyone if she reported the rapes.

In Michigan a group of more than 530 female prisoners filed a major lawsuit claiming sexual abuse by prison staff. Appalling as it is when women have been abused outside, it is outrageous for that abuse to continue when they are imprisoned. As early as 1995, the Department of Justice filed suit against the state of Michigan when nearly 100 percent of the female inmates reported being treated in a sexually aggressive manner by male guards. In 2000 a settlement resulted in policy and procedural changes. Male guards no longer conducted pat down searches of female inmates, and they no longer guarded females' housing and shower areas. More than three dozen criminal convictions of guards occurred as a result of the lawsuits. [7]

If females are victimized prior to incarceration, does it become a habit that persists in prison? Perhaps there is a pattern of exchanges made, and the prisoners are offered and receive favors. Or perhaps, like Jan Lastocy, they were terrified of receiving punishments that would lengthen their time if they did not comply with orders. Maybe they were afraid to speak up lest they accumulate more time spent away from their children, and they were cowed into silence.

Yet a local shelter for victims of domestic violence sends out information in the mail that insists, "Silence is not an answer." It tells of a

6. Isaak, "Scandal in Georgia Prisons," 6.
7. Weir, "36 Guards Convicted," 1, 5.

woman who left home with her son after a co-worker recommended the shelter. She had not told anyone of the abuse because she was afraid. At the shelter the woman received counseling and support for herself and her son that changed their lives. Now they can talk about their feelings.

When I worked at Florence Crane I heard a few complaints about sexual assaults, and they were investigated when they were brought to our attention. At the time I worked there, the women prisoners were open and more talkative than the male prisoners, but still I never heard them tell stories of victimization. Frequently silence and abuse accompany each other, and I wondered why the women were not talking. The next chapter tells about prisoners after their first day in a public works program, when they were quiet, sullen, and resentful. I was relieved when they began talking even though their frustration had more to do with exhaustion than fear of exploitation. But because the females used more words than the males did not mean they told us everything. Wordiness is not transparency, and the unspeakable cries to be exposed.

13

Ladies in Prison: Being All We Could Be

*I have probably been changed more than the people
I am supposed to be changing.*

—JEAN HARRIS: *STRANGER IN TWO WORLDS* [1]

A PALPABLE HEAVINESS HUNG in the room where forty female prisoners slumped on their beds at the Florence Crane Correctional Facility for Women. Their expressions were sullen as I walked into the minimum security unit we had taken over from the neighboring men's facility. This was the end of their first day on the Public Works program. They were required to be on their bunks and silent for count, but right now they were unusually quiet. I was conscious of every step I took. The prisoners had called me "Shoes Libolt," and I could hear my heels pounding on the terrazzo floors like hammers. I listened for the light soft-spoken comments, conversation, or usual grievances about actual or perceived wrongs. I was not prepared for this silence. I anticipated that the women might be animated about their first day on the Public Works crew after taking over the same work the male prisoners had been doing. Many of these women had seemed so tough.

I walked with the Inspector. The prisoners were more formal with me than they were with her. They enjoyed joking with her, and especially the attention she gave them. Today they greeted her with the same stony silence.

---

1. Jean Harris, "Pages from the Bluebook," 509.

I tried to engage a few by asking them about some specifics of the job. Later I was amused. Would male assistant deputy wardens ask male prisoners who looked resentful how their day had been? I could have let them stew in sweat and silence on their beds. Maybe I was crazy to care—the traditional "female" thing to do.

If their silence had not made such a statement, I might have enjoyed it—brief as it was. Though the females were less likely to fashion a lethal weapon in private and surreptitiously stab someone, generally they talked non-stop, sometimes using obscenities, screaming, laughing heartily, crying, and pouting. They wore us out, and many employees preferred working with more dangerous male prisoners than with the females and their dramatic emotional interactions and verbal onslaughts. Male and female employees who worked with the female prisoners became savvy and learned patience.

I was puzzled to hear employees who had never worked with female prisoners say it was easier work than working with the men. Some employees (men and women) talked about working in "real" prisons, referring to men's prisons at higher security levels. Others found out the hard way they couldn't resist seductive prisoners; even when the prisoners were willing, sexual involvement broke the law. One male supervisor at the women's facility seemed to view his work there as a temporary bump in the road until he could be promoted and work in a men's prison. Some female employees, too, seemed to think working in a male institution was the place to earn their stripes.

So I was relieved when one of the prisoners who had been on the Public Works detail responded to my question. "It was so hard working today." Another chimed in, "We worked like dogs." She looked as if she were going to cry. Yet I felt myself bristling. I quoted my mom. "Hard work never killed anyone." Mom lived her philosophy too, gardening, cooking, cleaning, and milking cows on our dairy farm. I wanted to tell these women how ungrateful they were, and how good it was for them to be working for better pay.

I was fortunate to have the opportunity to work with female prisoners. The work was the same as in other prisons, and the women gave me insights and perspectives I wouldn't have had if I'd worked only in predominantly male employee and prisoner work settings.

The medium security Florence Crane prison for women was located in Coldwater close to the Indiana border. It was a radical change from the men's maximum prison where I had worked previously, with its mostly male administrative staff. The first day at the women's facility, I made a remark to one of the supervisors about the predominance of female supervisors and managers, and she said, "Yeah, and it works damn well."

Part of my job entailed meeting with a group of female prisoner representatives to resolve issues on their agenda prior to their meeting with the Warden, to save her time. Their agendas were long. In addition to their verbosity, the women were, for the most part, articulate and adamant that they be given the same programs as the male prisoners. So I thought working in the Public Works program was a good opportunity.

Once the women's facility acquired the minimum security unit, separated from the medium security part of the prison, the women seemed enthused. Prisoners in minimum security could work out in the community on Public Work crews and make a better wage than in other prisoner jobs like working as a porter or in the kitchen. The women were being given an equal opportunity to take over the program. The jobs were the same and had not changed because the female prisoners would be doing them. The Public Works supervisors still needed prisoners to clean up the animal pound and crews for other projects like cutting brush and digging ditches. Public Works was an opportunity to give back to society and to show the community the female face of prison and how hard female prisoners could work. In addition, I anticipated the work with its higher wages would be a morale booster. The first day of work on the Public Works program the women appeared to have forgotten these benefits of minimum security and working in the community.

But once some of them began complaining, they weren't going to stop. One of them said, "We were in the mud and trenches. This work is too hard for ladies."

The "ladies" term was often code for what the women thought they should *not* be expected to do, such as more strenuous physical labor or jobs not commonly held by women. I was forgetting they were largely from an urban culture and unaccustomed to physical labor. Survival for them often had to do with adapting to a street culture.

I should have left then. Our discussion was not going to improve, and I wasn't going to convince them this work was good for them. Except for their mouths, every part of their bodies was tired and aching, but so far they had not raised their voices, and although they looked resentful, they seemed more resigned than anything else. I wanted them to have employment and career goals, opportunities that women couldn't take for granted.

Instead I said, "I've worked hard all my life."

A disgruntled prisoner said, "Deputy Libolt, you wouldn't do this work. If you had your period, you wouldn't be out there in the mud, using those outhouses for bathrooms."

"Oh, I have used outhouses," I said, but knew they didn't believe me. They saw me in suits and high heels with a management position, but I'd grown up on a dairy farm. In the summers my sister and I worked for farmers growing crops to raise money for school. We toiled beside migrant workers picking strawberries in June, raspberries in July, and string beans or cucumbers in August and only used the outhouses when we absolutely couldn't wait any more and then held our noses while we were in them—period or not. We never thought of staying home that time of the month.

Our work wasn't over at the end of the day either. No resting on a bunk: we had chores on the farm. We fed calves, helped Mom with the dinner, tramped grass in the silo, and drove tractor in the summer. Meanwhile Mom baked bread, and canned and froze food. Our allowance was what was served on the table, and we didn't ask questions. It was expected, and all we knew. But it was different too. It was temporary. I wouldn't do it all my life, and instead of returning to prison after a hard day of working in the field, we went home.

I'd read in the papers about a man who'd murdered his wife and was transferred to the men's prison where I'd last worked. One day I looked in his file. A relative had visited the prison, and made a statement. "I thought he'd be serving *hard* time." Did she think he'd work at hard labor? I imagined the chain gang under the supervision of an armed officer I'd seen in a southern state.

Years ago prisoners raised vegetables and cattle for their meat. The relationship between work and food was more immediate. The female prisoners likely did not know about that history. The women on their bunks behaved as though the Public Works program was both hard labor and inappropriate work for women. Their models of work likely had not been teams of women working on crews outdoors.

Another prisoner piped up. "It's like the army."

"That's right," I said. "Be all that you can be." It was time for me to go. Maybe they would be more positive after a good night's sleep.

Yet it dawned on me that perhaps I wasn't "being all I could be" either. I felt an affinity for these women and wanted them to do well, but their griping got under my skin. Sometimes I felt ill-prepared to help them. I wasn't good for them just because I was a woman. When I took the position at the women's facility, it was early in my career, and I worked with them only a short time before I was promoted and transferred to another prison. But they left such indelible impressions that I remember not only some of their first but also their last names. I see their faces to this day—probably because they exhausted me by being in my face so much more than the male prisoners.

I found myself sympathizing with the women. One woman who walked with a cane could have been at home knitting sweaters for her grandchildren if she hadn't killed her son-in-law because he was beating her daughter.

The female prisoners have often been victimized. Many have had difficult lives and then are separated from their children when they are incarcerated. Because of these conditions, though it was tempting to expect less not more of them, it was imperative for them to do something productive that could lead to a job once they were released. It may be easier to manage a prison where prisoners sit and watch television just as some parents use T.V. as a babysitter. But because of what they experienced we knew they were resilient and capable of more with the proper programs and treatment.

Sometimes women in prison discover they have choices, even if they don't initially enjoy what they're doing, like working at manual labor. They find they have latent talents when participating in a program or learning a skill or taking up art and discover how rewarding it is. The Michigan Department of Corrections provided meaningful programs designed to do more than reduce idleness. Though prisoners—and staff—do better in an environment where they are not idle, prisoners didn't count widgets to keep themselves busy. Some of the ideas for viable programs came from the women themselves.

One day I asked an unhappy and difficult prisoner what she wanted to do with her life. She wanted to get a Master's Degree and go to the

University of Michigan—"like you did," she said softly. Some of them learned to dream for the first time in prison.

However, much of the Public Works was harder outdoor work, and many of the women were ambivalent about nature. An ignorance and distrust of nature coexisted with a fascination and identification with it. I saw both males and females enjoying plants and flowers for their own sake for the first time in horticulture programs, a program typically reserved for minimum security prisoners. Dog and puppy programs offered at the other women's facility encouraged a love of animals and parenting skills at the same time. I was hoping the Public Works program, by having prisoners outdoors for more than sunbathing, would familiarize them with nature so they would experience it in a healthy trusting way.

Many of the prisoners had grown up in urban concrete settings without gardens, animals, or field trips. Sometimes the women didn't know how to respond to the "wildness" of nature creeping in where they lived. Their confusion was apparent one week when some of them saw mice in one of the dormitories.

Screams ripped through the night. We sent the Fire Safety Officer to remedy the problem, but a few days later the prisoners railed against us again. Female prisoners, some who had neglected or abused children, could not stand to watch the mice die so inhumanely on the sticky tape the Fire Safety Officer had left to catch the mice. Either they identified with trapped mice, suddenly sympathetic to a being as lowly as a rodent, or their reaction was a diversion from the routines of their lives enclosed in concrete and steel.

In *I'll Fly Away*, a female prisoner named Barbara Parsons, who spent time in a Connecticut prison and loved nature, writes about a prisoner "wide-shouldered, tough as nails . . . screaming like a sissy" because she and several other prisoners see what looks to them like a giant rat. She shoos the possum away and turns to see the "frightened faces of the girls, who from the time they were small children, witnessed the terrors of the streets."[2]

In 1981 Jean Harris was imprisoned in the Bedford Hills Correctional Facility for Women in New York for the death of the Scarsdale Diet Doctor, Herman Tarnower. In *Jean Harris: Stranger in Two Worlds*, she wrote that she once heard an inmate who knew all the scents of per-

---

2. Parsons, "Reawakening Through Nature: A Prison Reflection," 232.

fumes in bottles say, "What good is flowers? You can't eat 'em."[3] Jean Harris was often amazed by the inconsistencies of the other inmates—and staff. (Employees appeared inconsistent to her not only because their policies and procedures changed frequently, but because those policies and procedures were implemented differently by different employees.)

A large percentage of the prisoners had been prostitutes on the streets before coming to prison. Some studies estimate that as many as 70 percent of female inmates in American prisons were initially arrested for prostitution, about the same percentage who experienced incest and sexual abuse before incarceration. Yet some of these prisoners could hardly stand it when Prisoner Jean Harris walked around in her bare feet because, "You goin' get something bad on yo feet ef you don' get on yo shoes. Look at dat girl! She crazy walkin' roun' with bare feet like dat."[4]

Could working outdoors in the Public Works program give the female prisoners a healthy perspective about the world, instilling some respect for the beauty of nature while they learned that dirt and most bugs wouldn't hurt them?

Be all that you can be. So the Public Works program with its outdoor work clearing out brush from ditches and cleaning horse stalls looked like the army, though I couldn't imagine these women in the army. They seemed too soft. Yet many of them knew about life at its hardest in ways I didn't. But what did they have against physical labor? Did it seem beneath them? Did they dream of having some prince rescue them from all of this? Was there something deeper and darker like the fear of abuse? Had they already worked at menial jobs or seen their mothers working long tired hours as housekeepers or laundresses? Perhaps Public Works was a reminder of an unpleasant past.

Be all that you can be. Was I being everything I could be? I was persistent, determined, and disciplined, and I wanted the women to be disciplined in the way an army boot camp makes a certain type of woman out of us. Marching, in the trenches, in the rain and muck, following orders—Hup 2,3,4—Hup 2,3,4.

Yes, I knew that way, my way, out on the farm, picking berries, feeding calves and bucking bales. Perhaps if I'd worked fewer hours and smarter I could have been more persuasive with the women early on.

3. Harris, "Bedford Hills: Maggie Strong," 342.
4. Harris, "Pages from the Bluebook," 446.

I could have capitalized on their strengths quickly instead of trying to impose my values on them.

The women wanted to have their say on any changes affecting them. Considering their concerns and working with them gave me better results. Arguing was not effective. Female prisoners responded better when they were communicating back and forth with us, listening and talking things over in a process leading to understanding, even when the end result and answers were the same. They didn't do as well with orders unless there was an emergency. They were not much different from some employees, like me, who expected two-way communication.

When I told the prisoners "Be all that you can be," I was not yet everything a manager could be, but I became better because of working with the female prisoners. I worked to understand them as they became accustomed to working in the Public Works program.

The women gradually stopped complaining about hard labor. We also began to hear the positive comments about their work from community leaders and citizens. I heard someone say that the female prisoners were not as strong as the males had been but that they had more will. The women began to feel some pride about their work. By taking jobs they didn't always find appealing some of the women developed habits of work and work skills that men have traditionally had. I hoped they learned that all labor can have dignity, and hard, physical jobs can lead to work like that of the women who held management and administrative positions in the prisons.

Sometimes we must trudge around in the muck in our work boots before Cinderella's slippers fit. After manual labor, removing work boots and slipping your feet into high heels and cleaning up your fingernails is sweet, but it doesn't necessarily make you more of a lady than cleaning out horse stalls.

However, when they returned from working with their crews each day, I stopped short of telling the women they looked smashing in their work boots.

14

Kasey: Code 10

WHEN I THINK OF "being all we can be," I think about Kasey. I did not know her well, but I liked her. The people working in prisons who are defined as heroic have often saved someone's life. Kasey could have lost her life, but is one of those people who quietly go about making it possible for others to prevent serious incidents in a prison and perhaps in so doing save lives.

She was prompt and unassuming when I asked her to work on a radio problem, and she usually solved the problems, something a deputy warden appreciates. I knew about her past as a case manager and the path that led her to her work on the prisons' radios. There was an irony about what she did now, since it was a call on a mobile unit radio that may have saved her life.

Before repairing radios, she had worked in 8-block as a case manager counseling prisoners and addressing their concerns. Her conscientiousness and willingness to help others made her an excellent case manager in spite of a whopping caseload of 150 prisoners. She did not realize she was in one of the more dangerous prisons, until she got her "ass whipped," as she puts it.

It could have been different for her. A violent prisoner I'll call Brian Parker was elected block representative in her unit. As a prisoner representative, he had more access than others to her office to discuss the prisoners' concerns.

Over the years, and after serious assaults and a few deaths, policy and procedures had reduced and restricted prisoner movement and improved staff coverage, and serious incidents at some prisons. Yet a dangerous prisoner like Prisoner Parker who had a record of beating and choking a woman would have some freedom of movement, as he did when he was in 8-block where Kasey worked before she repaired radios. After all, it was hard to predict which prisoners could be violent, and his decent behavior while in prison led employees to believe he had mellowed or learned to control his anger.

One day Kasey learned that Parker had acquired illegal drugs, and went to the administration to inform them. But before he was busted, he found out her intentions. Finding that she was behind it, he was furious. He worked in the kitchen and confiscated a thirteen-inch rail from a food cart. Under the pretense of meeting with her about block concerns, he made his way to her office armed with his weapon.

Parker's anger propelled him across the desk, and he attacked and beat her with the shank. He also wound an extension cord around her neck. She screamed and fought back, but eventually lost consciousness.

Finally there was a commotion. Officers heard her cries and came running, but she lay on the floor bleeding, no longer able to take in her surroundings. An officer had called a code ten on his mobile radio, an emergency cry for help. Prison employees receive training for this type of call. Somewhere in the middle of the melee Brian Parker decided for his own reasons to stop his murderous assault, and Kasey survived.

The Corrections Department gave her time to recover. During her recovery she struggled with anger and the realization that she was not invincible. The wounds from the assault went deeper than the surface. Her illusion of safety was gone.

When she had nearly recovered, prison management decided not to give her back her old job inside the prison walls or any job within the prison. The assault had denied her a job she loved. She could have sued. A prisoner had attacked her, and she was no longer able to perform her job as she had known it. She did not file a lawsuit or a claim for lifelong workman's compensation. She asked her supervisors what she could do.

Kasey was working in Central Office when a supervisor asked her if she would evaluate the adequacy of our radios. She knew nothing about radios, except, of course, how crucial they could be in an emergency. The supervisor handed her a cardboard box full of radio parts, hardly "state of the art" technical expertise for radios so important to safety. Kasey took up the challenge. She read books. She made trips to the state police. She learned bit by bit and piece by piece, and developed the expertise she needed to service the transportation radios and to provide technical assistance to the arsenal sergeants for radios used in the prisons.

Her enterprise grew. She added a couple of technicians, and was given a shop in the countryside close to five prisons. She was named Radio Manager and provided assistance to all state prisons. She has saved the prisons a good deal of money because it no longer has to depend on outside experts for maintenance and replacement of radios.

She was asked to work on the radios at a time when radios were fixed on an informal basis or sent out to a contractor for repair. Radios are crucial to safety in a prison, and inadequate radios jeopardize security especially if they fail when a cry for help is transmitted.

Prisons are inherently dangerous places. The prison where Kasey had been a case manager was more dangerous than many. Staff were scattered and often only connected by radio. The prison air is webbed with radio transmissions: conversations about prisoner movement, transmissions about the availability of food service, mundane comments just to say that someone is there—the daily routine of prison life, punctuated not quite rarely enough by a cry for help, the code 10 that brought officers running to Kasey's office when she was assaulted.

I was intrigued with the transition she had made from case manager to radio manager. Had she repressed what had happened, burying it so deep that it wouldn't surface so she could go on with her life? Or, had she gone to therapy, faced the trauma head on, and somehow overcome it? Perhaps she was working out some kind of justice, as if weighing on scales what was done to her versus what good she could do for the prison. She seemed to come out of the incident somewhat triumphant.

I had been to the building where Kasey set up shop to work on the Corrections' radios only once before, so I asked her for directions. From the towers at the Jackson prison complex, I saw an expanse of unsettled land with some rolling hills stretching east to a stream and clumps of trees back to the radio shop with a rather makeshift one-lane road leading up to the shop on a knoll. The rutted road calls for a four-wheel drive vehicle, but I am bumping along in an ordinary sedan and will be taking my time to get to the shop. Thirty years ago the prison had farm camps of minimum security prisoners raising the prison's beef and pork on this land, but now the few buildings are empty and dilapidated. Sometimes farmers rent the land from the state, and we frequently see deer taking advantage of the cornfields along the road. This is desolate country, and I know I wouldn't be comfortable working where Kasey does especially during the months when it's dark both in the morning and at night. I wouldn't stay late. Not very many employees come out here. This is her base, but she usually goes to the prisons where the radios are.

The sun is higher, but I feel a chill and turn up my heater. In the prison where I spent most of my career, I rarely looked over my shoulder even though I could not afford to be complacent, and yet, strangely, I often was. I settled into the routines as many others did. Officers knew where I was. When I made my security rounds to check on conditions, employees, and prisoners, officers frequently radioed the post where I would next make rounds while I was en route. They even had a radio code to identify executive staff members making rounds inside the prison, and it amused me when I arrived at an officer's station before the transmission did, and the officer accepting the advance notice call had to say, "You're too late. She's already here."

I didn't kid myself. Many of those calls were made less for my welfare than to warn the officers at their posts to be at attention so they would look as busy as they often were. When I came to see them, they were on their feet.

Not everyone was watched like deputy wardens. The officers and case managers and others who interacted most with the prisoners were more likely to get hurt, and it seemed there were never enough officers to be every place they were needed. We tried to make certain we were not in isolated areas when prisoners were out of their cells.

I drive a few miles when the road turns and goes uphill toward the shop. Kasey meets me herself dressed in a brown jacket, blue jeans, and boots. She wears her dark brown hair medium length and in a casual style. She is slim and attractive with large light blue eyes, the color of highway chicory, and the air of a tomboy about her. I imagine her as a feisty cowgirl in movies of the romantically portrayed Wild West, or holding her own in a bar if things got ugly. I wondered if she would find it strange that out here I felt exposed and vulnerable.

She offers me a cup of coffee, and shows me the shop, introducing me to one of the technicians she employed. "I have saved the State vast sums of money because it is no longer necessary to depend on outside experts for maintenance and replacement of radios," she told me proudly. "I laugh when callers expect a forty to fifty-year-old white male instead of me, a woman," she said.

I came to her shop to ask about some radios. I had not intended to ask about the assault, but it seemed to hang there in the room. "Do you ever think about him?" I asked.

"Brian Parker," she rattled off his prison number instantly, voice raised. Other facts came rapid fire like bullets revealing the indelible impression left on her. She knows him in the intimate way you know someone when you're close enough to feel his breath and see the rage, knowledge not obtained from any record. Resuming her normal pace of discourse, she tells me there came a time when, for the sake of her sanity, she had to stop chasing information about Parker. All the facts in the world would not have healed the wounds, physical and mental, inflicted by him. Knowledge did not bring peace.

Before I thanked Kasey and left the radio shop, she told me she thinks other women working in prison delude themselves into thinking this could not happen to them. Like me, they may be more leery of driving down a lonely road in the country than working in a prison.

I thought of all the employees who have pursued litigation for real and perceived injuries. Kasey could have filed a workman's compensation claim and been paid handsomely the rest of her life. In fact, she was asked frequently, "How much did you get?" Instead, her question was, "What can I do?"

Justice is not always found through the courts, though we imagine we will find impartiality or some kind of resolution there. Kasey chose differently, not seeing the point in spending her life dwelling on her assault, getting even, or thinking of herself as a victim. Perhaps she is stronger or more resilient than many of us. She does not think of herself as a hero. Doing with what you have—in her case a cardboard box with radio parts and her initiative—is remarkable. Working with those radios is a form of an ironic justice. She knows there will be other Parkers, and that someday one of those radios she repairs will transmit a code10 and save someone else's life.

Later when I return to the prison, I hear the crackling on the radios when I make rounds in the prison. I think about calls for help that I receive—those other calls not transmitted on radios, and wonder if my responses to those calls made anyone's life better as a result. Sometimes while talking with prisoners, I know I give them weary looks. Did I pay attention when a prisoner told me about an abuse that had occurred?

I remember talking with employees too who came to me with problems. I remember asking, Are you sure this is a problem? Are you certain you're not overreacting? Sometimes there was no way to tell if I helped someone. I didn't know if I fixed anything. The terrain of management is full of ambiguities of judgments and questions without answers.

The physicality of what Kasey experienced directly—the assault, the call for help, and the assistance—struck me. Her work on the radios is as tangible as a slap. There's no mistaking it; either those radios are fixed or they are not.

15

Being Dorothy: Lawsuit

'Yes, said the Woodman, 'at last I shall get my heart.'
'And I shall get my brains', added the Scarecrow joyfully.
'And I shall get my courage,' said the Lion thoughtfully.

—THE WIZARD OF OZ

I LISTENED TO THIS prisoner tell me his crime was due to "being in the wrong place at the wrong time," the mantra I'd heard so many times. Did he expect me to believe it?

Of course, sometimes individuals *were* in the wrong place at the wrong time and are consequently now prisoners. Peter, only fifteen years old, was waiting in a van while two acquaintances went to commit an armed robbery but something went wrong, and they murdered two people. Although he had stolen the vehicle, he did not kill anyone, yet was held accountable for the murders. He was sentenced to life without parole.[1]

Committing no crime and further from home, Marat Kurnaz went to Pakistan to study Islam and left his German parents without saying goodbye, afraid they would try to stop him. While traveling with missionaries he was sold as a terror suspect to the U.S. military for a three thousand dollar bounty and spent two months in a prison in Afghanistan before being moved to Guantanamo Bay. He spent five years there even though documents from both Germany and the U.S. showed he was in-

---

1. Amnesty International USA, Group 81, "Thousands of Children in U.S. Sentenced to Life Without Parole."

nocent. In an interview with him, Amnesty International reports that the Germans thought he "slid into" his situation because of his "distinct naïiveté/immaturity" and because he was "in the wrong place at the wrong time." He replied, "Naïve, inexperienced? It was the Pakistanis and Americans who made the mistake...I am innocent."[2]

It's tragic when prisoners like Marat Kurnaz who are innocent are imprisoned. When prisoners tell me they were in the wrong place at the wrong time, regardless of how convincing the evidence looks I have learned to ask, "How could you have avoided being in that place, or what will you do when you're released to avoid being in the wrong places at the wrong times?"

Prison employees also can relate to wrong places and wrong times. I took a deputy warden's position at Birch Woods Correctional Facility (BWCF) a positive environment, only to see the environment sour. Sanford was a small town. The people welcomed the new prison and snapped up the jobs. I was sure I was going to the right place, but I was not there long before I moved to a position in another part of the state.

Some prison environments are hostile and unhealthy because of factors unrelated to the prisoners housed there. Employees joked that, yes, prisons were hard places to work where we had to "watch our backs," and dangerous—and that was only because of the other employees. At Birch Woods the reason for the distress was a new inexperienced warden, Marlene McCabe.

The popular Warden Camille Jarvis had retired. The stark contrast between Jarvis and McCabe was a shock to everyone. We all worked for the same department and used the same policy books. All supervisors and wardens were trained repeatedly throughout their careers to recognize hostile work environments and prevent them from occurring at all.

The behavior and attitude of the two leaders was remarkably different and accounted for the change. Jarvis looked for what each employee could offer in the workplace and used their skills while McCabe seemed to zero in on weaknesses, revealing them in an unflattering way. Jarvis listened to employees' creative ideas for the prison while McCabe made changes daily as though employees did not know she was the new warden.

2. Meroth and Rauss, "Five Years of My Life: An Innocent Man in Guantanamo," 8–10.

I experienced one of McCabe's strategies shortly after she came. She had invited her boss's boss, a heavy-set Mr. Welby, to come from Central Office. She called me to her office to meet with the two of them. The beefy Welby asked questions while McCabe sat silently, a smirk now on her usually distrustful looking face. The questions focused on our prison's practices when Jarvis had been the warden—angry questions that didn't wait for responses. When I left, I wondered if an attorney should have been present since the meeting was less about gathering information and more for grilling and intimidation. I was a bit amused by it all, too. The only "practice" they had forgotten was the bare light bulb hanging down from the ceiling.

While Jarvis knew she had authority, I realized then that McCabe did not have control of the prison. Welby had to visit to prop her up. Jarvis had never had to call in the "big guns" from Central Office to make her point. I had a good idea of how McCabe would treat other staff.

Employees' reactions to McCabe varied. Those who were targeted or felt discriminated against or harassed by her tried not to get noticed and endured what was happening, or transferred to other prisons. Some went on stress leave. Few filed grievances immediately.

The toxic atmosphere was creeping into the prison like the chemical contamination that had seeped into the Sanford land not far from the prison several years ago. The PCB poison-soaked ground was enclosed in a large field full of long grass fenced off with "Danger Keep Out" signs. Once when I took a wrong turn to Birch Woods I saw the land about the size of a city block in the middle of cornfields and flat pastures where cows grazed. I imagined chemicals leeching into the ground and the ensuing crisis followed by the posting of the red signs and the area declared a disaster. I wondered if anything grew there now, or if strange mutations of life had taken up residence in the wild grass.

This gated area wasn't the only reason for the economic downturn for the town, though it was ironic that another gated area, the prisons, promised a more stable future, not unlike other communities in the state that had benefitted from prisons. More prosperous communities often had a contingent of citizens who opposed prisons because of their concerns that property values could decrease and safety be compromised. Others argued that safety improved with the presence of additional cops in the community. Usually, expectations for employment in the community trumped a community's resistance to a prison.

Any opposition here at Sanford for the Birch Woods Correctional Facility had been half-hearted. Faded billboards greeted anyone driving off the highway into town, and a few ramshackle old businesses, signs of better times, stood along the old road on the way to the prison. With a new prison, business picked up for an old gas station, and an additional modern station opened downtown. The few Sanford restaurants were filling up again at noon. A renewed excitement was apparent in the town. The prison had attracted many employees who moved to Sanford and the surrounding area. Warden Jarvis attracted good employees. I would miss those employees.

An attorney was calling. I was not surprised the employees had complained. Several of them contacted me after I left, and told me about their interactions with Warden McCabe. They had filed a lawsuit.

While I was still working there, I didn't see the signs—at first. A few employees came to my office suggesting things were not the same or were not right, but I wasn't quite conscious of any specific problem, much as you're not aware of the spider crawling from its web on the ceiling down a thread until it appears in front of your face and must be reckoned with. Then an employee let us know that she would be taking a few weeks off to participate in a drug program, and the warden tried to "discipline" her. McCabe accused an employee who had missed work due to illness of lying. One day I heard McCabe use the phrase, "I'll be down their throats." Agendas changed dramatically and came from behind closed doors.

As the prisoners say, "I was in the wrong place at the wrong time" by the time I transferred from Birch Woods to assume a position at another prison. I didn't expect to hear much except for the occasional call from a friend who was still working there. The attorney who called was working on the lawsuit from employees, filed against McCabe.

The attorney said that everyone with whom he talked spoke of how miserable she had made them. They had been in tears as they related their experiences.

She looked uncomfortable, distrustful, and unhappy to the point of being grim. It would be unfair to say that she was all bad like a one-dimensional villain in a suspense movie, but her arrival, like a storm cloud, cast a black shadow over the yard.

The attorney asked me some questions about McCabe. I reminded him I had only worked a month with her before assuming another position. He told me my experience with her according to other employees in that short period of time was similar to what others had experienced. Employees told him she had undermined me.

Deception had taken over almost overnight—so suddenly it takes your breath away—like going to a strange fairyland where trolls and monsters appear at every turn. Few things remained predictable though prisoners were behaving as they usually did in minimum security, and we drove home after our shifts.

Employees' reactions to the environment and circumstances were also fairly predictable. In their eagerness to please and follow leaders, employees will overlook a leader's weaknesses as long as they are treated fairly and with respect. Wardens count on this loyalty. Employees will overlook a few mistakes if the warden doesn't know every policy. However, if employees feel threatened, they will leave or fight back.

Again, the attorney said he had never had a case like this—one where people had reported such misery—and he did not intend to "lose" the case. I had heard about his reputation of winning.

Employees who are favored see what is happening and fear becoming the next victims. Consequently they often engage in obsequious, fawning behavior toward the person they fear while alienating themselves from employees who are excluded.

Divisions cropped up. I was not there to see that happen.

The attorney said that employees had used the phrase, "in the car" to describe the environment at the prison. Have you heard of it? he asked me.

Employees had always gossiped about who had the favor of those in positions of power, and who would be promoted to desirable jobs. Those who had worked in Central Office, or played golf with higher level managers or did them favors, were familiar and more likely to receive promotions. Competency had little to do with who was "in the car" and more to do with who rubbed elbows with those who had the power to make promotions. I began to hear more about who was "well-connected" and less about who was a good manager and why. "In the car" was slang like the "in-crowd" in high school and referred to those who were favored. Employees divided into camps—favored and not favored, those "in the car" and those left out.

When I left I wondered about the employees who remained there. Managing a prison was difficult work for employees without worrying about whether they were accepted and valued by their leaders.

The last time the attorney called he told me this case reminded him of something his father had said. "The only way evil is allowed to continue is if good men do nothing." Then he asked me about "Dorothy."

"Did one of the managers call you 'Dorothy'"? He asked me.

"Dorothy? Not that I know of. What does it mean?"

"Dorothy, like in the Wizard of Oz."

"I don't get it."

"You know, Dorothy like being naïve."

Asking, naïvely, what it meant must have amused the attorney.

Except for the ditty, "Ding, dong, the witch is dead," I remembered little about the musical with Judy Garland, *The Wizard of Oz*, or the book. Being identified as a "Dorothy" and "naïve" should not have surprised me. I plead guilty. During my career I met employees who were distrustful in a healthy or "street-wise" way and often perceptive about the manipulations of prisoners and staff. They instinctually picked up on the games that both prisoners and employees played. Later an employee told me they were not going to tell me about being called Dorothy. I didn't ask why anyone thought I was naïve, but, of course, I was—naïve to believe we'd all be accepted as we worked at the new prison, naïve to believe what happened was unusual—and naïve in many other ways.

The attorney had allowed me to look through a crack in a door and see how poisonous the Birch Woods prison environment had become. And like Dorothy in *The Wizard of Oz* seeing her Kansas house whirl around, I stayed at my position just long enough to see the world of the prison begin to turn upside down. Dorothy likely had a dream, as many of the employees did—a dream of escaping. Only later did she realize she was in another wrong place.

Work in a prison is simultaneously risky and tedious. Complicated problems that defy simple solutions can blow up quickly like a tornado in the Midwest. We can be swept into strange worlds of adversity, and find ourselves in the wrong place at the wrong time where it's hard to believe we have what we need to make it through dark tangled forests of life. Like the Scarecrow, Tin Woodman, and Lion, we think we are not complete with what we already have.

Dorothy's ragtag band of inadequate, vulnerable creatures took a perilous trip to find they had a community. The charming story of their dependence on each other, each needing and offering something like the community in a prison, remains attractive for a reason especially for keen leaders who help vulnerable creatures figure out how they can best serve. A Scarecrow needs brains, but protects those at night who sleep. A Tin Woodman lacks a heart but can chop through trees and branches in the path on the journey, and a Lion while seeking courage can provide a strong back when the rest of them cross ditches—all on a journey to believing in themselves, connected, and no one left behind.

Naïveté believes we need something like an outside wizard and silver shoes to rescue us when in fact we already have what we need. The innocent and naïve may not fare well in prison. But when things don't go well, we long and dream for a better place—a place that has an Oz where odd folks come together to help each other out, a place where conflicts are resolved, lawsuits are not necessary, everyone rides "in the car," and witches disappear like magic.

Witches rising up and appearing again in different forms stirring their cauldrons of brew until they boil over, scorching their targets? In my naïve days I believed that women, a minority in a male-oriented environment, would help each other out. I didn't think women would take stands against one another—before working at Birch Woods.

At one prison an exceptionally gifted secretary worked for me. She anticipated what needed to be done and told me that she enjoyed her job and working for me. I transferred to a more established prison where I met what I thought was the secretary from hell. I tried to hide my disappointment, but my face must have revealed it all and often. Like the time she came in my office when I was meeting one of the managers, and she placed her hands on his shoulders, and rocked him back and forth, teasing him. I was puzzled by her distortions too. When I asked her not to make coffee in my office while I was meeting with other employees, she told others I wouldn't allow her to make coffee. When I told her she was not too old to attend college and encouraged her, she said I was discriminating against her due to her age.

When she filed her harassment complaint to a counselor, he contacted me about a "serious complaint." I had not seen it. We made arrangements for me to read it and speak with him. He was mystified after talking with me. I did not seem to be the person in the complaint. That's because I was not. The person who dwelled on the secretary's nicely typed out secretarial pages as though a spell had been cast on the paper, was a twisted image of me. The report picked up some of my words and turned them into ugliness. Was I a wicked witch? Or was she? Perhaps she and I were a mixture of double toil and trouble. But witches? One of the many unfortunate terms used to describe women who are feared or loathed has a sad history, and yet that term comes to mind.

The secretary had filed harassment claims before in hopes of making something stick followed by a stress leave or attempting to acquire some compensation for damages. I had my grievances about her too; she had performance problems. She received her last boss's e-mails and printed them out for him. He had teased her, and told her to "shut up." Did she trust him, or did she trust the way it had been?

Somewhere between the lines of the report was a person I failed to reach. Not a witch but a frightened, anxious woman who felt she couldn't tell me why I threatened her or why she couldn't work with me.

16

Style and Class

The courtiers had style but Queen Wilhelmina had class.
—SIETZE BUNING, *STYLE AND CLASS.* [1]

STAN DROBAK, A FRIEND and former Michigan State tennis coach, tells the story of a woman who came to see him about tennis lessons. She was dressed to the nines in a stylish, beautiful tennis skirt and matching shirt. Stan was talking to her about schedules, and times and dates for courts when she said, "Oh, the lessons aren't for me. They're for a friend of mine. I learned how to play yesterday." The woman didn't know much about playing tennis, but she was going to look good on the court. Her tennis balls may or may not find their way over the net into the next court, but she'd swing her racket in style.

I think of style as something on the surface, like a signature. If a person wears clothes and make-up of a certain kind typical of them, we say they have a unique style. A few years ago Tom, a high school senior, asked me to speak for his class about working in the prisons. We agreed to meet at the front doors of the large school. I arrived before he did and watched many students coming in through those doors. Most of the boys wore baseball caps with the bill in front, though a few wore their caps backwards. Long t-shirts and baggy pants completed their outfits, and soon they all looked alike. I said a little prayer, "Lord, help me recognize Tom when he walks in the door." Tom spotted me standing there looking lost, and we walked to class together.

1. Buning, *Wilhelmina,* 17.

High school boys (and girls) may not want to stand out so they conform. No policy at Tom's school required school uniforms, and yet the students' attire had few variations. Someone who wore a dark dress and pearls or a suit was obviously a teacher.

Demeanor is also style. The young prisoner in the following chapter stood out with style in an environment where it's difficult and not always safe to stand out. He was an individual who let me know no one was going to grind him down.

Some people adapt their style almost chameleon-like, fitting themselves to people they want to impress. Having a particular brand or make of car or living in a certain neighborhood and being a part of a certain crowd may change depending on whether it is to an individual's perceived benefit.

Having style is not the same thing as class, but the difference between the two fascinates me.

Some of us think we live in a classless society even as the evidence indicates otherwise. Increasingly people are divided into classes by occupation, race, and financial status. Most of us know equality is not reality. The poor and minorities, overrepresented in prisons, are on the margins of our society. Many have missing teeth and scars because they have not had access to health care. Many do not use proper English. Formal education may not be accessible or affordable to them. When released, offenders have records, making it even more difficult for them to enter the job market or make a decent wage. Like many people on the margins, they know others look down on them. However, as I've said before, prisoners are not the only ones breaking laws or harming society. I think of CEOs with grossly huge bonuses letting employees in their companies go. If only we could regulate greed!

Another meaning of class has less to do with social status than doing what's right or what's best, regardless of style. More than an attitude or how one looks on the outside, "class" refers to people who are confident they are doing what is right for others even if it does not benefit them.

Prisoners have been humbled. We do not think of them as having class, and yet many have a sense of dignity as they do their time. Wealth and possessions do not mislead them into thinking they have class, but many know what is right and best. We would not be able to manage our prisons without their work and cooperation. Prisoners who have had so much taken away sometimes have class.

My grandmother of Dutch extraction talked about people who thought they had *standt*, or special standing. She was fond of telling a story about a Dutch family living in her town whose money was on display in bone china, cloth napkins, their dress for dinner and other finery and outward accoutrements of *standt*. The family referred to a man who maintained their gardens as "the gardener" instead of using his name. In the Netherlands people were more likely to stay in the same stations and occupations as their parents. In the United States this casting is not so prevalent. When the "gardener" became a successful business man in a nursery, no one called him the gardener. They knew his name, a name his employers could have used long before he became successful. He may not have had style or class, but the family with style who employed him could have shown more class by using his name. An older poem about Wilhelmina from the book, *Style and Class* (1982) captures the difference between style and class in a light, humorous way.

Wilhelmina

Queen Wilhelmina
was entertaining the Frisian Cattle Breeders' Association
at dinner.

The Frisian farmers
didn't know what to make of their finger bowls,
They drank them down.

The stylish courtiers from the Hague
nudged each other, and pointed, and laughed
at such lack of style.

Until the queen herself
without a smile
raised her finger bowl and drained it
obliging all the courtiers to follow suit
without a smile.

The courtiers had style
but Queen Wilhelmina had class.

—Sietze Buning[2]

2. Buning, *Wilhelmina*, 17. Used with permission.

17

The Dazed Gaze

His gaze has from the passing of the bars
grown so tired, that it holds nothing anymore.

—RAINER MARIA RILKE.[1]

MANY OF THE YOUNG prisoners who came to the youth Reception Center were coming to prison for the first time, and they were scared. As I read their files and asked them questions, they were wary, not only because of questions they'd likely answered before, but also because they were worried their responses could land them in a prison worse than the one they were envisioning.

The employees and I used terms like "assessing" and "processing" interchangeably for the paperwork and the prisoners, one going with the other, as we prepared the prisoners for transfer to the prison appropriate for their security level. Once all the paperwork was complete, and a bed was available, usually in a few weeks, they transferred. We were fond of saying that if we didn't like a particular prisoner, he wouldn't be with us long. We were the sorting factory for the youth sent to prison. In their identical loose-fitting blue uniforms, they must have sensed their similarity to the cogs on a moving conveyer belt of some machine in a factory.

We didn't have many choices about where to send young prisoners. Based on their ages, length of sentence, and the type of crime committed, they would go to the prisons identified in policy which met those criteria. I had been told interviews with them prior to their transfers were

1. Rilke, *Der Panther*, 30.

important, but sometimes they were a formality and luxury. Sometimes we didn't have time for an interview, and the paperwork was completed in the prisoner's absence because the county jails were sending us more prisoners, forcing us to transfer prisoners out quickly. Every four to six weeks our population turned over, and a sea of new young faces received picture IDs, prison blues, and a hygiene kit.

We struggled to find beds for prisoners in other facilities since most of the prisons by policy did not accept prisoners unless they were twenty-one. Still others preferred taking older prisoners so we were always fighting for beds, begging other prisons' employees to take our prisoners. Our exchanges were passionate.

Because we had received more prisoners from the county than we'd expected and were in need of a bed, I called one of the transfer coordinators at the end of a particularly long day.

"I thought it was going to be my wife on the line for me," he said.

"Well, I'm not, but I need a bed," I replied. We both laughed as I reminded myself to be careful about my word choices.

One afternoon the officers brought a young man to my office for his interview. He did not look scared or docile. He wore his blue uniform as though it had not come out of a box from the factory, but something he had chosen and tailored for himself. He was wiry and not a lot taller than I am. He may have noticed my jaded look. I may have suppressed a yawn. Classifying the young men could be deadly on a summer day after lunch. As I read his file, I began asking him some routine questions. Suddenly he began talking louder. He looked directly at me. "You think I'm like every other prisoner."

"What?" I looked up from his file. He looked directly in my eyes. Perhaps he knew we had few choices about where to transfer him. He didn't seem worried I'd transfer him to the Upper Peninsula, our equivalent of Siberia with its long winters and distance from urban areas and family.

"Yeah, you think I'm not much." He was talking faster. "You think I'm not smart?" Not waiting for my response, he said, "You'll see. I'm going to be an attorney. I'll do well."

Even though he had my attention, his interview didn't take long. He kept giving me "what for," and talking as he walked out the door. In that unguarded moment I felt some affection for this young kid with cheek, and shame for my numb weariness. I followed him trying to tell him I hoped that he would do well, and become an attorney if that's what he wanted. He walked out, bouncing from one foot to the other, feisty the whole time.

With a criminal record, he was going to need some spunk to become an attorney once he was released from prison. I often think of him reminding me he was not "piece" work. I hope he did well, but I'll never know. I don't remember his name, but his chutzpah roused me from my dreary lethargy that day. It was as though he climbed off the conveyer belt, had on different, tony clothes, and made himself visible. He had style.

Rilke's poem about a tired gaze, and an enclosed space holding a force, deadened, and thousands of bars describes a panther pacing in a zoo. Of course the images are evocative of cages holding subdued prisoners too. I hope the young man retained his spirit in spite of being surrounded by bars and that "his gaze" unlike Rilke's panther didn't "become so tired it held nothing anymore." Even pacing in small circles often stops in prison, and in too many the light goes out of a large spirit including those of employees who notice inmates only when they cause problems.

When we are numb, prisoners blend in with the landscape. Employees look past them to talk with other employees. Prisoners working at jobs that keep the prisons operating smoothly often stop making eye contact with employees. Prisoners in minimum and low medium security planted, weeded, and watered flowers in the prisons. They served food in the prison dining rooms and cleaned the prison inside and out. They cleaned our offices, and received training to clean up blood spills. For the most part they cleaned well, the way we expected them to clean. They were paid a little, and having a job was a diversion from their cells. They did the manual dirty jobs we didn't want, and we didn't always recognize them when they did a good job, typically commending the employees who had trained the inmates if the unit was particularly clean. We expected the work and yet the inmates were invisible. We treated them as a mass and walked by unless they had questions or got themselves noticed in some negative way. But the tasks they completed kept our prisons operating.

Nancy Ortberg from the Menlo Park Presbyterian Church in Menlo Park, California worked at one time as an emergency room nurse and tells of how one doctor talked with another about Carlos who was completing menial functions. Nancy relates witnessing the following conversation.

> "It was about 10:30 p.m. The room was a mess. I was finishing up some work on the chart before going home. The doctor with whom I loved working was debriefing a new doctor, who had done a very respectable, competent job, telling him what he'd done well, and what he could have done differently.
>
> Then he put his hand on the young doctor's shoulder and said, 'When you finished, did you notice the young man from house-keeping who came in to clean the room?' There was a completely blank look on the young doctor's face.
>
> The older doctor said, 'His name is Carlos. He's been here for three years. He does a fabulous job. When he comes in he gets the room turned around so fast that you and I can get our next patients in quickly. His wife's name is Maria. They have four children.' Then he named each of the four children and gave each child's age.
>
> The older doctor went on to say, 'He lives in a rented house about three blocks from here, in Santa Ana. They've been up from Mexico for about five years. His name is Carlos,' he repeated. Then he said, 'Next week I would like you to tell me something about Carlos that I don't already know. Okay? Now, let's go check on the rest of the patients.'"[2]

I'd like to think the new doctor stopped to look at the faces often ignored and moved to the background. Maybe he opened his eyes and his gaze took in Carlos. At least he knew his name was Carlos while I can't remember the name of the prisoner who made me take notice of him.

---

2. Karlgaard, "His Name is Carlos," no pages.

18

Seeing Red: The Rug

[T]he consummation of work lies not only in what we have done, but who we've become while accomplishing the task.[1]

— David Whyte

Every job is a self-portrait of the person who did it.

—Anonymous

Style without class is a sounding gong and tinkling cymbal.

— Sietze Buning[2]

ONE MONDAY I HAD the rug pulled out from under me—literally. Sometimes clichés, instead of standing for some broader principle, are narrowed down and rolled up into one event.

The Warden stood at one end of the Warden's office and I in the opposite corner, a visible indication of how far apart we were.

"When were you going to tell me I was wrong?" he asked, and for the second time I found it hard to speak. I wanted to ask why anyone needed to tell him. Why didn't he know? He had worked in Human Relations. The employees called him "Mr. Personality."

At the job before I'd taken this one, I had a small oriental rug with black and gray designs on a cream colored background with touches of an ambiguous crimson, coppery color often seen in oriental rugs.

1. Whyte, "Courage and Conversation," 5.
2. Buning, *Style and Class*, 116.

Surfaces are hard in prison. Everything is metal or cement and the paint colors are often drab. The rug brightened and softened the gray linoleum tiles in my office. The floors in the office at this prison were the same gray, and the rug dressed up this office too.

The warden had first laughed about the rug. When he came into the office with male supervisors, he joked about the color in the carpet. He made remarks referring to it as "pink." He also commented on the pink message cards someone had given me as a goodbye present at my last prison job. He told me he didn't ever want to get one of those notes from me or anyone else. I didn't take this seriously. I had already seen the inadequate number of prisoner and cell shakedowns recorded, the lax documentation in logbooks, and the closet doors left open to caustic/toxic supplies. Our facility was not always complying with policies. With all the issues to manage in prison I couldn't believe he would be bothered by pinkness. But there were other things, too.

He had not chosen me for deputy warden and thought someone else should have had the job. He didn't realize that sometimes wardens don't choose, but that Central Office staff sends deputy wardens who may complement a warden or be a good fit for that prison. He told me he'd *had* to take me from the western region of prisons in the state. I'd not heard that one had to stay in his or her own region for promotions, and he had come to this prison from another region. One day he told me he didn't think I'd intimidate staff enough. Wardens and deputy wardens made policy-required inspections of the prison. He frowned about doing inspections. "I'm your policy," he'd said. "You need to cultivate some snitches so you know what's going on. If we're out in the facility, staff will be uncomfortable and not perform the job the way they usually do." Wardens were not necessarily knowledgeable because they were wardens. That's why wardens and deputy wardens worked together. Ideally, they worked as a team. Maybe he knew all that and was making outrageous comments to get a reaction from me.

I should therefore not have been surprised to find my rug rolled up and leaning against a corner of the lobby by the door one day. He had let me know before that he didn't think I belonged. He was not subtle.

I told myself to keep my perspective intact. In the scheme of things, this was not a major catastrophe. And yet, I couldn't speak for a few hours, I was so angry.

When the warden asked to see me around noon, he told me he'd had the rug removed because he had concerns about my style. He was worried I wasn't tough enough. I found my voice. I defended my work, and told him about my accomplishments, something I typically found unnecessary. He admitted he had never heard otherwise. Then I told him I would not intimidate people. I left his office still shaking.

Finally, I called a colleague, Sherry, whom I trusted and who knew him. Others talked with me too. They had heard about the rug, and told me he was wrong. Denise, the Regional Administrator also found out. During the next few weeks the warden asked to see me, and asked when I was going to tell him what he did was wrong. Someone in Central Office had spoken to him about the rug. Some higher up leader had "chewed his ass." Colleagues had spoken with him too. He had worked in Human Relations in Central Office and knew the words about hostile environments and discrimination, and yet unless someone told him he didn't seem to recognize that yanking something out of a colleague's office may not be right.

I wondered how I'd brought out the worst in him. If I'd been tough in his way, as he described it, perhaps I would not have felt victimized. Long ago I heard a woman who leads seminars on abuse tell people to stand and say, "Tell, tell, tell." Pulling up someone's rug was not abuse, though I was puzzled about why people would not tell someone if they had been harassed. But before the warden removed the rug, there had been a pattern, as obvious as the geometric pattern in the rug that I'd ignored. He had been derogatory and arrogant, and I made internal excuses: this must be the reality here, or maybe he'll change. I didn't want to believe what was happening so I did not speak up. Others did not seem to be targeted, so perhaps it was just me, and I could correct something in my "style." I didn't need that rug in my office. For a short time I kept his behavior a secret, and the shame of it simmered below the surface like hot ashes from a smoldering fire.

I thought of a beautiful female officer who worked on second shift in my unit at a previous prison. When the administrators left the facility, other officers on her shift made it difficult for her. If she radioed a message, some officers made loud noises so her voice and transmissions couldn't be heard. She spent some time communicating with prisoners, and her fellow officers called her a "social worker." She was anxious about how staff treated her but asked me not to tell anyone about it because she was afraid that being considered a snitch would be worse. Soon she couldn't concentrate on her work, and her attendance suffered.

I was afraid too. I did not trust my instincts or my colleagues and friends though I knew when people behave like bullies they should be stopped. Bullies know as surely as a dog senses vulnerability who they can intimidate. But I was not a helpless victim who needed rescuing. If I'd admired the warden, I might still be thinking I was the problem, but I didn't. I remember the warden's question so well, not because it is written in my journal, but because it is my question: *When were you going to tell me?* When was I going to say I would not tolerate this? He deserved that. Worse than yanking up an employee's rug is sweeping under the rug whatever's amiss and hoping for the best.

By writing this, I'm not trying to settle any scores. Although I don't respect that warden, I don't dislike him. The reason I'm writing this is because of the shame for the way I behaved. I'm sorry I didn't stand up to him and for what was right sooner. I'm sorry I didn't go to the Regional Administrator and tell her what happened before someone else did. Denise was there to help and didn't see me as a troublemaker, another fear I had.

Denise didn't become an administrator by taking easy routes herself, but she always had a sense of equanimity and elegance. I had noticed her shoes and purses often matched. Her office was decorated with lovely pictures and photographs. She had style. I wondered whether she had ever been questioned about how she decorated her office.

How we decorate our walls and what we wear tells others about what we value. As I worked with her, my perception sharpened. She was not there to decorate the environment but to "paint" it with fresh ideas. Her focus on the work and knowledge of the details of prison administration impressed me. When I met with her I had questions, and she not only answered them, but had additional ones. She saw the big picture too. She had also worked in prisons where the composition of the administrative team was entirely male.

During her career in Corrections she worked to include minorities and women in the Corrections environment. She was fair and concerned about justice in all the prisons where she was an administrator. Her artistic bent extended to the Corrections environment. She had style and class.

One of the employees I supervised was completing what he saw as the more physically active and glamorous parts of his job while he neglected the details, perhaps too mundane for him. His office was disorganized, with papers strewn about. What caught my attention was the picture on his wall displayed prominently for anyone walking by to see—a group of men in military garb, a front row of them kneeling, and a back row standing, all glaring at the camera, looking tough as though to say, don't mess with us. The caption on the picture was the quote of the character Harry Callahan, played by Clint Eastwood in the 1983 film *Sudden Impact*, "Make my Day." Perhaps the picture didn't offend anyone. I didn't say anything. The picture is part of the lore that was the past culture of Corrections telling of strong courageous men and the times they subdued enemies, in this case disruptive prisoners. The war stories provided the fodder telling us that we fought valiantly and overcame the foe. There are other stories to tell.

Shortly after the rug incident, I went to a women's criminal justice conference in another state. After I registered, I went to my hotel room to take a nap and fell into a deep sleep. I had a bad vivid dream. I panicked, struggled from the covers, and ran to the door to make sure it was locked. Sometimes we don't recognize our distress until, unbidden, a dream shakes us awake. The next day at the conference, a woman who was a judge spoke about whiny women who complained about harassment and didn't seem to know which battles to fight. Most of the women I knew who eventually complained "knew which battles to fight." Sometimes they didn't say anything until their stress became unbearable. I was thinking, "tell, tell, tell."

Whenever I took a new position in a prison I asked myself if I'd be able to do what was right and if it was the right place for me. You may not think you can do your work effectively, but it may not be practical or even possible to transfer even when your environment seems so wrong. In this case, I realized I could have worked with that warden. He was misguided rather than cruel. He made his awkward amends. He even asked to come with me to do inspections. He moved on to a promotion. A colleague told me he was "well-connected" to those who promoted employees. I stayed, and the employees who were some of the best with whom I worked, were respectful.

I had heard the cliché about learning from bad leaders, and I learned from the rug incident—some broader principles. Clichés, like "having the rug pulled out from under you," can mean one temporary setback and not that you don't have a place to stand when you know what's right.

If your boss doesn't support you, your employees will be inclined to think they can undermine you too. When prisoners know, as they often do when our own behavior is not as it should be, safety is compromised. If we cannot be good examples and models for prisoners, everyone is demoralized. Some bosses use different standards of behavior for those they supervise than they do with their superiors or colleagues.

I also viewed diversity differently. More than a workplace with women and minorities, to me diversity is about accepting those with different styles. During my career I have interviewed many people for positions. Some of them had pizzazz, flashiness, or sophistication. Most did not. They didn't always have the "expected" style of employees often seen in prisons. They were not necessarily people of large stature or assertive voices, or people who had served in the military or with police backgrounds, or those with political connections. Many were good employees, not so stylish but with substance—and class.

A few years ago I read about the warden's motivating keynote address to new Corrections officers, men and women, "challenging them to do their best, learn as much as they can, and embrace *the ethical standards* necessary to become well-rounded professional corrections officers." I wished he had defined ethical standards in his speech. I hoped it wasn't a cliché. I thought about him in his perfectly pressed suits, gold bracelets on his wrist. A man of style.

I tell stories, the ones about fighting battles, as much a part of the prison culture as other war stories. I tell others about Denise who saw the details making up the large picture. I remember her office which seemed to say that prison administration is an art.

When the warden transferred to another prison, I was the acting warden for several months at the prison—one of the oldest prisons with a long history. A friend who stopped by to visit me walked through the two secretaries' offices to reach mine. He smiled and said, "Adria, in the past some big butts sat in that chair." We laughed, but when he left, I realized that I was always sitting on the edge of the large leather warden's chair because if I sat against its back, my feet wouldn't touch the floor. I had the chair from my old office sent over. The chair was comfortable, just my size, and the upholstery was various colors of crimson, red, pink, and vermillion, colors that brought out the color in a rug that lay on the floor of my office at one time.

19

Getting the Right Information
and the Information Right

*The place God calls you to is the place where your deep gladness
and the world's deep hunger meet.*

— FREDERICK BUECHNER[1]

The work is only our work as long as it is the right work for us.

—DAVID WHYTE[2]

DREW WHITLEY WAS INNOCENT by a hair—not a hair's breadth, and not his own hair, but another person's. He had served eighteen years of a life sentence for the 1988 murder when six hairs found in a stocking mask allegedly worn by the killer were found to contain DNA that didn't match Whitley's. In the last few years other similar stories have emerged, and people convicted of murder and rapes but long claiming their innocence have been exonerated because of the DNA left at a crime scene.[3] People like Kirk Nobel Bloodsworth, who in 1993 became one of the first men exonerated after being wrongfully convicted of rape and murder of a child. [4]

---

1. Buechner, *Wishful Thinking: A Theological ABC*, 95.
2. Whyte, "Keats and Conversation," 235.
3. Moushey, "DNA Evidence Excludes Whitley," no pages.
4. Miller, "Looking Askance at Eyewitness Testimony," 1.

DNA's presence and power to exonerate innocent prisoners, some of whom have been on death row, has had a positive impact on other investigative practices, improving them significantly.

When I was hired as an analyst for the Corrections Program Bureau to evaluate educational and treatment programs in the prisons, I was not in a crime lab examining hairs that could lead to the exoneration of someone like Drew Whitley though sometimes I felt as though I was examining minutia as small as hairs. But DNA is not the panacea the innocent (but accused) and those in prison crave. And, of course, there is not always DNA. A drive-by shooting leaves no perpetrator's blood, semen, or hairs for examination.

When I began my analyst position, the promise of combining evaluation and educational and treatment programs intrigued me. I believed evaluation and research were essential ways to learn new things and improve existing treatment programs and systems. My projects in the Program Bureau included evaluating the effectiveness of the prisons' academic program, the classification program, and the prisons' psychotherapy program. I anticipated discovering information that would help ensure prisoners were receiving effective program services. My work gradually became a struggle, not because the work was not important, but because the work wasn't for me.

Before I could even collect data, I often had to work with those managing the educational and treatment programs on keeping records in a way I could extract meaningful information from them. Once that was in place I would be able to examine the records to see if prisoners were receiving the services recommended for them when they were sentenced.

Part of my work consisted of extensive interviews with many employees. The interaction with those who could most benefit from the evaluation is valuable for several reasons. The dialogue with these employees kept my evaluation from spiraling out of a practical context and losing its relevance. I often called on a person a second time to clarify what I had documented the first time or ask another question which gave me a richer perspective of the response, a way of replicating the information. Evaluation worked best when I was immersed in it with those who were giving me the information. I like the term "poking and soaking." The conversations with staff kept me from isolating myself from an understanding of the community that was the source of the information.

From interviews, I found many variations in records and how programs were delivered. For example the therapists used different methods depending on their orientations even though they were all holding prisoner groups for assaultive offenders and sex offenders. Some used cognitive approaches while others were committed behaviorists. Even when the therapists used the same approach, the program was not uniform. They used different techniques. Some psychologists were also more charismatic than others. Not surprisingly, answers to my questions varied, too. I asked questions like: does the psychotherapy program have an impact on prisoners' behavior while they are in prison? How long does it take for them to get into the program from the time they are sentenced, and if they transfer to another facility, can they easily resume the program? The responses to these questions varied. One of the recommendations I made for the psychotherapy program was that it be standardized so that prisoners transferring from one prison to another would be familiar with the program at a different facility.

The data I gathered for the academic programs was along the lines of determining what academic grade level prisoners were at when they arrived at prison, and if they progressed to higher grade levels as they participated in the prisons' schools. Are prisoners getting their GEDs more likely to find jobs when they leave prison? Does program involvement have an impact on prisoners' recidivism?

Sometimes the best I could say was: maybe for some, but I'm not sure what other variables may be related to success. Perhaps one could talk about a chain of events that occurred because a prisoner received a GED, and because of it found a job, and because he was working, did not commit a robbery or assault someone, but it was a stretch to say that academic success was responsible for the positive impacts and reduced recidivism. Whether programs or evaluation of programs saved lives was even more difficult to determine.

Searching for the right answers can be tedious and arriving at results time-consuming. We wouldn't know this from watching popular television programs in which crimes often appear to be solved quickly with drama and élan. Heroes and villains are a part of these crime shows like the western cowboy programs before them.

Criminal justice programs in colleges often attract students because of these forensic shows. What isn't often revealed in such shows is the careful work that occurs when gathering evidence or the analysis of drugs and other evidence in the labs behind the scenes. Investigating demands thorough procedures, which are all the more crucial when lives are at stake, but important for any type of study.

Ann Gordon, a forensic scientist in the Lansing, Michigan area, claims there are multiple disciplines involved with her job and that like all research it is painstaking. A hard look at all the details is essential.[5] Coming to a conclusion or determining what happened takes patience which can only benefit a process with so much at stake, particularly when the goal is eliminating innocents as suspects, and determining the guilty. Sometimes the best we can conclude is that someone is likely not the offender.

By its nature, evaluation research often proceeds slowly especially when the urgency of finding who committed the crime is not part of the study. As I mentioned, I was not examining hairs in a laboratory or the number of angels that could dance on the head of a pin. Taking some time to examine data is a luxury one doesn't have when there is political pressure to convict someone. But, sometimes I waited too long for answers that didn't come in the way I expected. Information must be gathered and weighed. I never felt as though I exhausted mining the data or making the best use of it. Had I included the best information? What had I missed? Was I really finished when the report came out or did I fail to consider additional information once I had written the report? The findings, too, as with many studies, including some with DNA, may show what is *not likely* rather than what is *true*.

Employees I had interviewed were courteous but didn't call begging for final findings or reports. Some of the employees viewed research on prisons as impractical and expendable in a way that riot gear is not.

Students that I taught in a criminal justice class at a local community college also did not find principles of research very relevant for their lives. They viewed topics of correlation and causation as subjects to be endured. To them the null hypothesis seemed like the dull hypothesis. When I introduced what an experimental study was, many of them who were concerned about what would be useful for them as Corrections Officers did not consider it relevant until I reminded them how we de-

5. Patzer, "Fighting Crime With Science," 46.

termine what medications are useful, why certain ones are preferred, and why we have more confidence in some than others. I learned to begin with those medication examples.

What I recommended was more related to improving systems and processes than actual research. It was modest and preliminary, not dramatic or glamorous. One report asked teachers to keep better records so that prisoners transferring to other prisons could continue their education by making a smooth transition into another prison's school. Another recommended that therapists, who worked independently using a variety of approaches, establish measures to assess change and effectiveness for rehabilitating prisoners. It was important work, even when I couldn't get past the idea that all the variables and details were not going to save lives or drastically change them. The uncertainty of funding threatened by state belt tightening also haunted me.

Research wasn't always popular but its positive effects on how the prisons operated were obvious. Some of the best programs and practices did not exist until research or evaluation studies recommended a program or system.

It's hard for me to imagine how prisoners were classified for particular prisons without an objective security prisoner classification system. In Michigan and elsewhere now, certain prison variables like past offenses, ages, and length of sentence indicate what level of security is likely best for each prisoner. This classification system conserves resources and enhances security by placing prisoners with less time in minimum security and those with longer sentences and more serious crimes in more expensive and higher security prisons regardless of how harmless they look. It may not be flawless, but security classification is a system based on evidence and has the potential to save lives.

Other recent preliminary studies show that reentry programs for ex-offenders may reduce recidivism, indicating they may be safely managed in community placements. This finding has the potential to make good use of precious resources by increasing focus and intensity of supervision on citizens returning from the prisons and keeping some people in the community, while reserving prisons for more harmful offenders who can't be safely managed in the community. Studies like these are too valuable to ignore.

My work in evaluation was some of the best preparation I had for working in prisons. In several prisons where I worked, I carried out investigations. I was accustomed to discovering what happened and finding the best answers partly because of my prior work in evaluation. Doing inspections and completing audits to make the prisons more effective and maintaining standards of accountability made use of the skills I had acquired in evaluation. Sometimes when I was working in the prisons, long after my work in evaluation, I couldn't resist asking if we shouldn't do a little study to determine this or that. My experience had become an indelible part of me, not altogether different from the way habitual offenders' prison sentences become a part of them.

Taking positions in the prisons and leaving the evaluation analyst position behind was the right decision. I was not that good at it. One person said it more directly than others, "You don't look like a researcher." Working in program evaluation and rubbing elbows with those in research was better for me than I was for it. I am indebted to the program bureau for allowing me to work there.

In *Crossing the Unknown Sea*, David Whyte writes about our sense of belonging in the work world. His own experience led him to believe we sometimes work at something that is not who we are while keeping our deepest desires for our lifework a secret, until something deeply humiliating or a loss of some type occurs. David was working in a corporation, keeping very busy and speeding through his work, never stopping to give himself or others any attention. One morning when hurrying from one task to another he saw some of his colleagues about to start a meeting. He didn't see the person he needed to talk to in the room, but put his head in the doorway and said in a loud voice, "Has anyone seen David?"[6] Everyone was stunned and then burst out laughing. He was the only David working there. That moment of humiliation sent him on a road to recovery from exhaustion and a new career of writing poetry. I did not want to wait for my soul to cry out and ask, "Has anyone seen Adria?"

It was difficult for me to admit I didn't like my work when the evaluation team around me seemed to be having such a good time. I also had obligations and was receiving rewards and payment. I was fearful of what would happen if I left the work that wasn't really for me. Others might have envied me having such a position, but I began to feel like a caged animal in a four-by-four-foot cubicle. I had yet to discover that working behind the walls of a prison was not as confining. Prisons are

6. Whyte, "The Awkward Way the Swan Walks," 124.

hard and sometimes frightening places to work, but I was made to do the type of work found there.

Even though I left evaluation work, I think some of the treatment programs and processes were stronger because of my studies and recommendations. What I took with me on the path to the prisons was a way of thinking, and those approaches and methods of analyzing information stay with me like DNA.

20

Prison Escapes, Inspections,
and the Cowboy Way

IN 2006, RICHARD MCNAIR, a convicted killer, escaped from the U.S.
Penitentiary in Pollock, Louisiana. He had escaped prisons three times,
and was the first prisoner in thirteen years to escape from a maximum
security federal prison. A bulletin went out saying he was considered
"extremely dangerous."

According to Mark Singer in an article entitled "Escaped," in *The
New Yorker* of October 9, 2006, McNair (in his late forties), was described
as good-looking, very likeable, and intelligent. His father said he digests
what he reads and remembers it. But McNair hasn't had a working life
because he's been in prison almost two decades.

A police officer in Louisiana had been notified of the escape from
prison in the area, and shortly after, saw a jogger running beside a rail-
road track. The car's video cam recorded the officer's pleasant conversation with McNair outside of his police car for about ten minutes. The
officer asked for I.D., but understandably the jogger had none. After being questioned, the jogger told the officer where he was working. At one
point, the officer laughed amiably and told the jogger he matched the
description of the escapee. The conversation, which may have seemed
long to the jogger, finally ended with him saying, "You have a good day,
now," and the officer replying, "Be careful, buddy."[1] By the time the officer tumbled to the fact that his conversation had indeed been with the
escapee, McNair was long gone. The police officer did not realize that
McNair, who acted his part as the jogger perfectly, had snookered him,

---

1. Singer, "Escaped," 46.

until Bureau of Prison (B.O.P.) officials watched the tape of the escapee with the officer.

Prisons have steel bars and hard metal, and often several fences with razor sharp concertina wire on top. Some prisons look like fortresses. How do prisoners escape? They have escaped "low" like three inmates who escaped from an Indiana State Prison in 2009 by going through tunnels that led to a manhole cover on a street. They have escaped "high" like Dale Remling in Michigan who broke out of prison dramatically in 1975 when a helicopter flew into the prison yard and picked him up. He was a fugitive for thirty hours before he surrendered to police. He said it was worth it because "he got to hear some birds sing, water trickle, and a fox bark." [2]

Most prisons have mission statements stating that protection of the public is primary to their operation, the *sine qua non* of their existence. Training consists of preventing serious incidents like prison riots, hostage takings, and escapes, all incidents that threaten to undermine that mission. Any time safety in a prison is jeopardized, people are in harm's way. But prisoners outnumber staff, and those prisoners with the most serious offenses and lengthy sentences are often desperate to escape.

In the early 1980s two desperate Michigan prisoners, one serving life for first degree murder and an armed escape attempt, and the other serving four life sentences for first degree murder, escaped from Huron Valley Men's Facility where I was working at the time. Both prisoners were working at their jobs in the yard picking up trash when a food truck entered the compound and picked up an unarmed officer at the gate, a normal practice. When the truck reached the loading dock of food service, the inmates pulled homemade knives on the officer and driver. The officer jumped from the truck and radioed for help while the prisoners commandeered the truck and told the driver to head for the fence. They crashed through the first fence before stalling in the soft ground at the second fence. Shots were fired, a bullet left a hole in the windshield, and employees surrounded the truck. Fortunately, no one was hurt.[3] Two desperate men had watched for their chance at freedom, but like Pharaoh's army trying to cross the Red Sea, they became too bogged down to cross to the other side.

2. Wyatt, "Peek Through Time: Reminiscing about Dale Remlings great escape," no pages.

3. Oppat, "Fence foils escape try at prison," Ann Arbor News, A1 and 4., n.d.

One of my responsibilities entailed responding to the media when they came to question us about a serious incident like this one. I never looked forward to their questions. The day of the escape, news reporters from Ann Arbor and Detroit contacted us and arrived in cars and vans with the names of their newspapers, radio, and TV stations identifying them. Our world that often seemed arcane and curtained off from the one outside the walls became a place open to the scrutiny of the public. Like hungry wolves on the prowl, the reporters devoured sensational news as desperately as the prisoners escaping sought their freedom. When speaking to the media, I tried to slow down and choose my words carefully. I'd been misquoted before, and—worse—actually used the right words and found them taken out of context. Once it's down in black and white, there's no asking for it back and the public may draw its own devastating conclusions about the adequacy of their protection. That day I was pleased to report that employees stopped two prisoners from escaping.

Richard McNair was described as highly alert with keen powers of observation. He seems to have escaped on his wits, and stayed out because of his charm. Patrick Branson, a deputy warden at the North Dakota State Penitentiary, a maximum-security prison where McNair spent five years and escaped, said that "McNair is a con man who is very calculating and patient. One of the questions he will be asking himself immediately when taken into a police car is, 'What's the weak spot in this facility?'"[4]

Richard McNair found those spots in prisons and made several ingenious escapes. Although many prisoners may not have the patience or acute intelligence to find the glaring or subtle weakness, or actually escape, many ask the question. Officers and employees may be employed to watch, but prisoners watch everything too. At least, employees are wise to assume they do.

Inmates watch for the loose ceiling tiles that may lead to an unsecured vent or door, maintenance doors to tunnels if prisons have them, and the way employees handle their keys. They listen to the radio traffic about where employees will be locating, or whether there may be breaches in the outside perimeter and inner fence security systems. They see into closets which hold caustic and toxic substances when employees have them open, or work in areas where employees lock up tool cribs

4. Singer, "Escaped," 46.

and notice isolated or understaffed areas and inadequate monitoring. In 2009 Arkansas prisoners escaped from a high security unit in jail by putting on jail guard uniforms made at the prison.[5] Inmates detect weaknesses in employees also and are tuned in to the employee who can be bought. They notice and will maneuver themselves into any chink in the armor.

In December 2010 in Georgia, prisoners, usually not very successful at organizing, managed to communicate their grievances by cell phones which were contraband. One prisoner paid an officer $400 for a phone worth $20 on the street. The prisoners ended the strike themselves within a week.[6]

What happens when prisoners riot, take hostages, or escape? There may be a hero. Maybe an employee saves someone's life or trips a prisoner on his way out the door, preventing an escape. One attempted escape from Huron Valley Men's Facility was stopped when an officer shot a prisoner as he was attempting to go over the fence. Most critical incidents like hostage takings, riots, and escapes are prevented daily by careful monitoring. According to one Michigan warden, sometimes incidents occur without an obvious violation or "red flag."[7] Prisoners have an abundance of time on their hands to think about escaping. McNair escaped by shrink wrapping himself and rearranging supplies on a pallet to hide himself in a cavity. He devised a snorkel-like tube as a means to breathe. A truck drove the pallets to a building outside the prison, and he broke away.

But unlike McNair's, escapes often occur in a less complicated way when opportunity comes knocking. An employee leaves a handful of keys or a maintenance tool unattended, and a desperate prisoner seizes his advantage. When investigations report those gaps, policy and procedure are revised to close them. An employee who has violated a rule or broken a law is disciplined.

Initially officials from the Indiana prison where two prisoners escaped through the tunnels "were tight-lipped."[8] Following an investigation, three officers were suspended for careless guarding of the prisoners. A governor in Arkansas called the escape there "inexcusable" and five

---

5. Montaldo, "Two Killers Escape Arkansas Prison," no pages.

6. NewsOne.Com, "Georgia Prisoners Use Cell Phones," no pages.

7. Runk, "Warden says no 'red flag' ahead of escape attempt," 1.

8. Martin, "Ind. prison officials investigate escape as 2 still on the run," 1.

officers entrusted with guarding the entrances and exits to the prison were placed on unpaid leave. [9]

In Michigan following an escape in 2005, audits found that prisoners' locations were not always documented.[10] In some reports about counts taken of prisoners, officers recorded them in two locations, and sometimes they could not locate prisoners. They found one prison was not keeping lists of critical or dangerous items moving in and out of the facility which meant that tools or items left inside the prison could be used to escape or fashion weapons. Some of the lists of tools and other items were left unsigned by the person bringing the items into the facility. Others had no authorized supervisors' signatures on them. One Michigan prisoner, who eventually attempted escape, completed a blank form he took from his counselor's office and arranged his own transfer to another facility.

I have mentioned that sometimes the hardest part of employees' jobs is the busy but mind-numbing routine of daily life in a prison. The day-to-day monitoring so important is not glamorous or exciting. It is not readily apparent that lives are saved by employees' watching and inspecting. The important work of keeping radios repaired that I wrote about in another chapter, is not the stuff of heroes. The officers who complete their required prisoner shakedown searches each day and find homemade weapons may not receive praise because completing shakedowns is "expected." Daily tool control and monitoring of prisoner movement are not the stuff of accolades either. Good officers are also attentive to well-behaved prisoners and win their confidence, so they know what prisoners are thinking and saying, the groundwork that can prevent an emergency.

Some employees, less concerned about the details, wait, coiled up and ready to strike, for the serious critical incident and the opportunity to act and react. I heard many of them flattering themselves and others for their toughness, bravery, and courage and patting themselves on their backs when they quelled incidents that could have been prevented in the first place. Some employees even neglected, ignored, or egged on prisoners who struck out for the fight the employees wanted all along. Even employees who were promoted to supervisory and management positions sometimes craved action, and looked for the chance to insert

9. Montaldo, "Two Killers Escape Arkansas Prison," no pages.
10. Bailey, "State audits cite slipshod tracking of prisoners."

themselves into hands-on combat with prisoners that officers were responsible for resolving. One deputy warden responsible for making decisions during a prison fight ripped off his glasses instead and joined the fray to break it up. My friends and I sometimes dubbed those employees who were hungry for physical action as "cowboys" (and "cowgirls"), an analogy to part of the work real cowboys and ranchers do.

My father-in-law was a cowboy in his youth. When he recounted how difficult it was, he smiled about dime store rhinestone cowboys with pretty boots and cowboy hats. He grew up in rural South Dakota, and as a young man went to work for the Diamond A Cattle Ranch, completing tasks that required skill and hard work. Long after his experience, he lassoed a pig once to the delight of his son. Cowboys were not the romantic stars we see on our television screen, and the work was the hardscrabble, dusty kind that made him glad to see the chuck wagon and flop on the bunk for the night before the drudgery began all over again. No maidens in distress were available for rescue from other companies, and there were no cowboy enemies to shoot. Mundane concerns like roping and branding cattle, and watching for rattlesnakes, coyotes, and prairie dog holes that could break a horse's leg occupied their time.

Like cowboys, good employees and officers in prisons look for the small signs of neglect mentioned above that can develop into serious critical incidents. Like sheep herders watching for predators, monitoring and inspecting consumes most of their time.

Early in my career in Corrections, I read the article in the March 1982 *Atlantic Monthly* on "Broken Windows" that spawned a movement in policing and making neighborhoods safe by chipping away at the chaos that typically precedes crime in the community. Not only do small drips from a ceiling become large leaks, but they reveal an owner who doesn't care. On a larger scale graffiti in public places breeds more graffiti when left unpainted. When graffiti is removed or painted over, the neighborhood seems to prevent it from occurring again. If a window in a city building is not repaired, others will be broken. Disruptive and disorderly behavior will also proliferate if left unchecked.[11]

As a result of the "broken windows" theory, policing changed from responding to a crisis to responding to a community's problems. Police, including officers in Flint, Michigan came out of their patrol cars and became familiar with people in neighborhoods who had been living in

---

11. Kelling, "Making Neighborhoods Safe," 46–52.

fear when people with undesirable behaviors moved in and destroyed property. [12]Not all police were convinced that this approach worked. Robin Kirk of the Houston Police Department said, "Traditionally, police officers after about three years get to thinking that everybody's a loser. That's the only people you're dealing with. In community policing you're dealing with the good citizens, helping them solve problems." [13] Becoming familiar with the people in the neighborhood and focusing on the good people in a community prevents chaos and corrects disorder. As a result, everyone is safer, the neighborhood and the police. "Broken windows" theory has been put into practice in the New York subways where order was restored by maintenance and by the presence of the police.[14] It worked in 1984 when a Virginia apartment building was repaired and taken back from drug addicts who had taken over vacant rooms.[15]

So when I took hold of a door handle on my first day at one of the prisons and found it sticky, when I noticed that the floors were dull and the unit was dirty, when I found officers congregating in groups rather than making their rounds, I thought of "broken windows." I set about getting to know the officers who supervised the prisoners who did the cleaning and went with them while they made their rounds and completed their shake-downs. I learned so much from them, how their work varied with some completing work thoroughly and others skimming the surface. Not everything was solved or wonderful for me. I was accused of sacrificing security for hunting down dust bunnies, and being a "city girl" who didn't understand priorities in a prison. One kitchen supervisor told me there was dirty dirt and clean dirt, and he had clean dirt. The employees were mostly trained to take action in a crisis—not supervise prisoners cleaning a floor.

I wanted to work in a clean place with people—not cockroaches. Officers had prisoners complete the housekeeping chores they found less "manly" when more action-oriented responsibilities were not demanding their time. A balance of taking care of what look like pesky details and tackling serious incidents like fights and escapes, showed prisoners we were paying attention and watching everything. Seeing obvious re-

12. Ibid..
13. Ibid., 52.
14. Kelling and Coles, "The Promise of Public Order," 1.
15. Wilson and Kelling, "Making Neighborhoods Safe," 1.

sults never goes out of style, and "what works" must be apparent. Mario Paparozzi writes "the fact is that when results do not matter or are invisible, one can do anything." [16]

Back at the ranch, cowboys on saddles straddle the routine and inevitable active work of herding and branding cattle and the work that requires quick almost instinctual responses. When my father-in-law was not tying knots and watching for coyotes, he broke wild horses, a ballsy activity associated with glamour but marked with inherent risk.

In prison when the routine was punctuated with a disturbance or fight between prisoners or an assault on staff, I was relieved to see strong burly officers like lions spring up, their faces red with excitement, the sweat of adrenaline on their uniforms, muscling their way to the crisis, *sans* guns. I was grateful they were trained to prevent escapes, break up fights, and pull prisoners out of altercations and apply handcuffs, reining in violence when it erupted—like cowboys and cowgirls. Some of them waited for these moments, and I knew this was their world while I stood by like a lame ranch hand. I liked hearing them tell how they had taken hold of this one's arm, and brought another to the ground while pinning his arms behind his back—as though they had gone to battle. When I wasn't within earshot or had gone home, they would talk about how they were the "real" employees here, and how we manager types couldn't do without them—and they were right about that last part.

Whenever the dust settled and the posse rode off into the sunset, I saw clearly how important it is to trot steadily and carefully, watching for rattlesnakes and prairie dog holes, but also how vital to gallop in fast when corralling wild horses or stopping escapes.

16. Paparozzi, "Much Ado About Nothing: Versus What Works," 31.

21

Reentry: Prisoners in Reel Time

SOCIETY'S ANXIETIES ABOUT PRISONS are often expressed in popular culture. Concerns about capital punishment surface in movies like *The Green Mile* (1999) and *Dead Man Walking* (1995). In *Shawshank Redemption* (1994), themes of the institutionalization of prisoners and the prisoner as hero dominate. *I Have Loved You for So Long* (2008) is about an ex-offender who struggles to adjust to the community after fifteen years in prison. The protagonist Juliette, played by Kristin Scott Thomas, experiences inner turmoil and harbors secrets. The film also reflects society's more recent focus on prisoner reentry—from prison to the community, a topic frequently covered in the media of late.

In the movie Juliette has served her time of fifteen years, but she is not the typical offender released from prison, not even typical for Nancy, France. She did not have a history of offenses or help from various social agencies and last chances in the criminal justice system until interventions were exhausted. Nor did she commit a series of petty or more serious crimes that frustrated judges, until they sentenced her to prison. She likely had a decent home life and no mental illness or diagnosis of "inadequate personality." Many people committed to prison come from lower socioeconomic classes and would not be particularly interesting on the screen unless they were magically made so by artistic film direction. Juliette has had economic and social advantages.

It's not that people like Juliette, who was a physician in the movie, don't go to prison. One evening in the late '90s when I was working at a prison in Jackson, Michigan, Dr. Jack Kevorkian was delivered to our doors from the county jail to serve his sentence. He had become infamous as a pathologist who claimed he had assisted 130 terminally ill patients to commit suicide.

The prison where I worked was built in the old style of several floors of open cells, tiers stacked on top of each other like those often shown in T.V. programs and movies, making it hard to keep him out of sight as he was escorted to his cell. In more modern prisons, notorious prisoners can be placed in enclosed cells where the prisoner is not so easily seen by other prisoners. Here the other prisoners saw Dr. Kevorkian handcuffed and escorted to his cell, and recognized him from newspapers and T.V. The chant began with a few voices, slowly, and then reached a crescendo. Soon a chorus of "Dr. Death, Dr. Death" filled the housing area.

Physicians like Juliette and Dr. Kevorkian go to prison along with drug offenders, engineers, computer analysts, and attorneys. They don't necessarily have an easier time than anyone else in prison.

The educated, celebrities, and the infamous are not always the easiest prisoners to manage, and their status may make it difficult for them to blend in with other prisoners or acquiesce to authority. They may convey, without trying, that they are smarter than the officers. They may show their contempt or superiority over other prisoners. Prisoners may detect their arrogance and prey upon them, sensing their disadvantages in adapting to the prison environment. They may become as institutionalized as any of the prisoners. Prisoners vary in resiliency, but prison is an equalizer and when they are released, they have many of the same needs as any of the prisoners. Juliette in the movie has a difficult transition back to the community.

I had occasion to see Dr. Kevorkian on several occasions when I made routine inspections in the prison. He looked small, pale, and weak. With its hospital, our prison was an appropriate facility for him. After his term, and release, he was not allowed to practice medicine, and he likely faced some of the same problems all ex-offenders face when they return to the community. Ex-offenders, with or without an education, like Dr. Kevorkian or the fictional Juliette, face the stigma of having prison records.

We see Juliette try to find a job. One potential employer, when he discovers her past crime, sees her as a monster. We watch her navigate access to social agencies and struggle painfully as she relies on those agencies and parole agents to find work and gain her independence and finally move to her own apartment. Her story and others occur daily and yearly in our society as prisoners try to resettle in the community. In the movie we see her face often taking up the whole screen. Though large numbers describe our prisons and prisoners, and ex-offenders returning to our communities, we can't look away from their faces. Reentry is personal. People returning from prison need supportive people.

The U.S. has the largest prison population of all countries. While globally the average rate of incarceration is 145 per 100,000, in the U.S., it is 762 per 100,000 [1] imprisoned or held in some type of court supervision. Jim Webb, the senator from Virginia who introduced the National Criminal Justice Commission Act, says that with 5 percent of the world's population and 25 percent of the world's known prison population, "we either have the most evil people on earth living in the United States; or we are doing something dramatically wrong." [2] Most prisoners will eventually be released to the community, 700,000 per year is one estimate. [3] Many are drug offenders, non-violent offenders, or mentally ill, and serve an average of five years. In Michigan, a large prison population has increased costs but not reduced the crime rate. [4] In fact falling crime rates may not have much to do with the criminal justice system either, but other facctors such as involvement in community organizations, churches, as well as discipline and values. [5]

Costs of incarceration, cited at anywhere from $29,000 to $32,000 per year for a prisoner compared to the costs of $1,250 to $2,750 a year for community placement, undoubtedly fueled the dramatic shift in focus from incarceration to supervision in the community, especially for non-violent offenders with shorter sentences. In addition, in a depressed economy, philosophy marries rational economic concerns of less expensive community placement as more ex-offenders are provided with structure, resources, and intense supervision to help them succeed.

Supervision can now occur at greater distances than in the past because of our monitoring technology. Agencies assisting ex-offenders who can be safely managed in the community with counseling, substance abuse treatment, housing and employment, ease their transition to the community. Add to that initial research showing the success of these programs, and a new emphasis emerges on reserving prisons for

1. Innes, "The Simple Solution for Reducing Correctional Costs," 32.
2. Perkinson, "The Prison Dilemma," 36.
3. Travis et al., "A New Era in Inmate Reentry," 38.
4. Kime, "Filling Prisons doesn't reduce the crime rate," 11.
5. Garland, *The Culture of Control*, 33.

the most serious offenders and the promise of supervising more offenders in the community.

The Michigan Department of Corrections, faced with a declining economy, developed the Michigan Prisoner Reentry Initiative (MPRI), an offender reentry model that develops a plan for prisoners to follow during their incarceration and prepares them as they are released. This program has reduced costs by having some prisoners, who have served their minimum sentences, supervised more intensely in the community. (MDOC has also closed thirteen prisons.) The prison population has declined 7 percent since early 2007 and has saved $500 million since fiscal year 2002, according to another article on the MPRI.[6] The program has also had a positive impact on recidivism.

Approximately two out of every three people released from prison in the U.S. are rearrested within three years of their release. Just over half return to prison because of a new offense or a violation of their terms of release. But with MPRI, parole revocations are down 42 percent since 2002, and jail intakes have declined 10 percent in 2008.[7] The MPRI, according to the Michigan Department of Corrections Administration, reports a 29 percent reduction in Michigan's return to prison rate.[8]

Recent articles about other states' similar reentry programs also examine the specifics of reentry programs and their success at maintaining safety, reducing costs, and reducing recidivism.

The Federal Bureau of Prisons reports a shift of focus from program participation to competency of skills for the best results. [9] Identification of core skills, assessment and measurement of skills acquisition rather than just offering someone a program to complete is preferable. Linking skills to reentry needs, allocating most resources to prisoners with the greatest skill deficiencies, and community information and collaboration all assist offenders as they make a transition to the community.

In a Minnesota program the most effective aspects of reentry were vocational training, work release programs, drug rehabilitation, halfway home programs, and prerelease programs. Lower recidivism rates were

6. Engle et al., "An Examination of Four States and Their Budget Efforts," 43.

7. Ibid.

8. Caruso, "Operating a Correction System in a Depressed Economy: How Michigan Copes," 37.

9. Breazzano, "The Federal Bureau of Prisons Shifts Reentry Focus to a Skills-Based Model," 51.

found in work release programs, day reporting centers, and home incarceration programs. [10]

Before prisoners can attain skills or participate in programs, they often have to overcome barriers such as getting a driver's license, a social security card, or picture identification. An ex-offender may be accepted in some program or obtain a job, but what if he has no ID or transportation to take advantage of it? Helping offenders overcome these barriers is also important for reentry and transition to the community and employment. [11]

For more information about a variety of community based reentry programs, see *Corrections Today*, December 2009, and February, 2010. Many of the articles on reentry report similar findings. Ex-offenders who have housing, work, drug treatment programs, and supervision in the community will likely have a more successful reentry than those who are not employed or in programs, according to most studies. Few would argue with those recommendations for ex-offenders, though not all ex-offenders have access to those programs.

One reentry survey of 2006 that particularly caught my attention questioned prisoners about what their worries were about reentry, and asked prisoners who returned to prison what they thought led to their reincarceration.[12] Though the sample taken of the prisoners was not large, 68 percent worried about reentry, but 76 percent didn't ask prison officials for help. Other worries cited included hanging out with the wrong crowd (53 percent), alcohol and drugs (45 percent), using transportation (40 percent), obtaining a driver's license (35 percent) and making new friends (25 percent). In 2006, 26 percent worried about finding employment, a figure that may have increased in the last few years of higher unemployment. For those who returned to prison, 40 percent identified hanging out with the wrong crowd as a reason for returning while 37 percent identified drugs and alcohol as reasons for their return. While reentry programs and agencies are essential, these surveys may indicate the need for mentors and supportive people in the lives of ex-offenders.

The movie, *I Have Loved You for So Long* is timely because it takes an unflinching look at the turmoil ex-offenders face, even as papers are

10. Hesse, "A Snapshot Of Reentry In Minnesota," 64.

11. Beeler, "Reentry: A Matter of Public Safety," 19.

12. Braucht and Bailey-Smith, "Reentry Surveys: A Reality Check," 88.

signed releasing them from prison. What they've done, what their lives have become in prison, and what changes they will be making require more than programs and agencies. The protagonist Juliette is prickly and uneasy. She does not trust people, and she knows they don't trust her. Reentry takes time, but family and new friends stand by, accepting her, being honest and non-judgmental.

On the MPRI website are reports of ex-offenders who talk about people, mentors, and friends who care about them, and stand by them. Not surprisingly some of those supporters are from churches. The Bible is full of commands to visit prisoners and help poor and needy people. It would be interesting to see to what extent having supportive people in their lives contributes to ex-offenders' and MPRI's success.

One parolee who prayed for a mentor said, "She encourages me, and she doesn't judge me."

A pastor who is a mentor said, "It's staggered us how hard it is for prisoners to reenter society, from work to transportation to finding a place to live. I see why people go back, because our society builds walls."

Another ex-offender says of the mentors, "They reach out and check on you. You don't walk in as a convict. They see you as a person."

Not all ex-offenders are in the Michigan Prisoner Reentry program. Other ex-offenders are discharged without supervision or are no longer under the supervision of Corrections. But they also need seamless access to various agencies, all kinds of help, and people who care that they make a satisfactory adjustment back to society.

At the end of the film in a dramatic moment when others accept Juliette for who she is, she says, "I am here." Many other ex-offenders in our communities are here in our communities and need resources, services, and agencies. They stand a better chance if mentors and friends reach out to them. No abstract principle led me to want to help ex-offenders—only people I met face to face, like Jaime, Isaac, Larry, and Monica. They convinced me to be there for them.

When I retired from the MDOC, I did not anticipate helping ex-offenders, working with them, or seeking their friendship. Sometimes looking at all the prisoners incarcerated and their needs overwhelmed me, and I assumed I would feel the same about ex-offenders in the community. Friends from Corrections talked about "moving on." So many opportunities in the community appeared interesting. My friends are from my church or from work, or have similar interests. I thought I didn't know many people who are poor, though we sing "Come You Poor and Needy" in church. Then I realized that ex-offenders are often poor and needy.

I had plans. I returned to a community college to teach. I volunteered for Meals on Wheels and joined Zonta, an organization for professionals that works to improve the status of women in the world. I decided to make use of my Master's Degree in education with a background in secondary remedial reading. I trained and then volunteered as a literacy tutor. I took a part-time position as a tutor/student coordinator at Capital Area Literacy Coalition, a non-profit agency in Lansing. I continued to jog my four miles every other day, and tend a large flower garden in the summer, and then there are evening meetings, some at church. I was soon as busy as I had been working full-time in Corrections. I told myself that the busyness was the equivalent of being useful.

Some of the students coming for tutoring to the Literacy Coalition were ex-offenders. Another man came to my church and recognized me. "I didn't know if I wanted to go to church where the deputy warden was," he'd said. We laughed about it later, but I was not as available or "present" for people asking for help as I could have been. It was that feeling of being overwhelmed. How would I ever help? I was not trained.

It is not uncommon to feel weighed down in any agency where people need so much. At the literacy coalition when I train the tutors I tell them to get to know the adult students and what their goals are before they prepare lesson plans. Many of our students are isolated because of illiteracy and are unable to participate fully in our culture. When I see all the needs they have I don't know where to begin. I do the best when I focus on the particulars of who is in front of me and what motivates them.

We are not asked to save everyone coming in the door, and we cannot make someone successful. When I worked in the prisons, I worked in one of them at a time. I supervised a team of people—not everyone in the prison. I worked on solving the employee and prisoner problems that came to my attention. I worked with who came before me, and whatever was my responsibility. My world was a small manageable circle.

In my garden the plants that thrive don't need my attention. Those that need tending let me know. Their leaves droop or turn yellow. I'm not always effective with them. Sometimes I don't know if they need fertilizer, water, or more sun; sometimes nothing I do is right and they wither, but I never work on the whole garden at one time.

People from our church who have an interest both in visiting prisoners and helping ex-offenders have come together to be a welcoming place for ex-offenders. We try to get to know these ex-offenders as individuals. Needs may be similar, but they are not all alike.

We have had some training, and we have rules. For example we know there is accountability when we work together. Private relationships with ex-offenders typically are not healthy and can lead to manipulation that is less likely to occur in a group. In addition we know that a group has knowledge of more resources than one individual. We have goals and expect ex-offenders to have goals. But we are realistic. We know that we can't help every ex-offender become independent, and we know we do not have all the solutions for difficulties that ex-offenders face. Sometimes all our team does is stand by and support a person who has come to us, and hope we will find ways to help.

I did not expect to work with ex-offenders. Perhaps it sounds strange to you to hear me say this, but I felt I had no expertise. Yet I found that the people returning from prison, needy for community as well as the basic necessities covet our support. Their faces are on our screens in real time.

22

Prison Ministry: The Word
in Concrete and Steel

"I did not come to bring peace, but a sword."

—MATT 10:34

FEW OFFENDERS RELEASED FROM prison want to return, even tempo-
rarily. But Isaac did to volunteer.

I was a deputy warden of six camps in the southeast region of
Michigan, and Isaac was a prisoner in one of them. I noticed him because he was leading a Bible study group for prisoners during his stay at
the minimum security camp. He smiled and was friendly when I made
my rounds, maybe because he wouldn't be there long before he was
released.

He told me that when he first came to prison, he felt abandoned
and alone. A volunteer named Norm who knew Isaac's family visited
him and Isaac's family in the community. When Isaac was about to be
released, Norm recommended a church for him. Neither of us knew it
was the church I attended. I was surprised to see Isaac again, but not as
surprised as he was to see the deputy warden in church.

Isaac's youth with an alcoholic father had been difficult, and prison
was hard, but the transition from prison to the community was especially challenging. Isaac was not the first person to tell me that release from
prison can be more difficult than going to prison. Prisoners do not make
most decisions about meals, housing, and activities, and suddenly when
they are released those decisions become the ex-offender's responsibility.
Finding employment, particularly if a person doesn't have marketable

skills or higher education, is daunting enough without worrying about meals and stable housing too.

A concerned family from the church helped Isaac make the transition to the community, and it was challenging for all of them. Soon Isaac found a good job and remarried, but he could not stop thinking about the men in prison. He remembered how alone he had felt. When he was paroled, he asked if he could volunteer in a prison. I had left my job in the Camp Program and was working as a deputy warden in the Riverside Correctional Facility's Youth Reception Center. Soon Isaac and his wife Marlene, both talented singers, began leading worship services and Bible studies for the young men committed to prison who came into the Reception Center. Our church's prison ministry grew when other volunteers from the church accompanied Isaac and his wife to the prison. The prisoners began to write Isaac and Marlene letters about what a positive impact the Bible studies and ministry had on their lives. One wrote, "Because you and your wife come here, I know I'm not alone." When I asked Isaac why he returned to prison to minister to the men, he said, "When a person has been forgiven much, much is required." I thought of Matthew 25:36.

Everything seemed to be going so well. He and his wife had a daughter. I wrote about his ministry in *Frontiers of Justice: Coddling or Common Sense?*[1] I thought he would be one of the ex-offenders who did well in the community. He'd be included in the statistics of those who succeeded and didn't recidivate.

But that was not the end of Isaac's story. He committed another crime. Fortunately, he was placed on probation and did not return to prison, but he'd never be able to volunteer in the prison again. His ministry to the prisoners was over, and he wouldn't be able to work at what was his passion—a loss for the prisoners as well as for him.

What looks like success to us may be quite fragile. Charismatic ex-offenders may be eager to preach or to discourage others from committing crimes or to take a ministry when they are not ready to lead in this way. An ex-offender, Lennie Spitale in *Prison Ministry* cites the "one year rule," and advises ex-offenders to wait for at least one year before engaging in a public ministry.[2]

---

1. Libolt, "The Pastoral Work of an Ex-Offender," 112–16.
2. Spitale, *Prison Ministry: Understanding Prison Culture Inside and Out*, 254.

Ex-offenders will struggle. Prisoners leave prison with many of the same problems they had when they entered. In addition they are institutionalized, stunned by changes in the community, and now have the stigma of having prison records. One friend says, "if you weren't crazy going in, you will be coming out." If someone is neglected or abused as a child, the boundaries of abiding by the law may not come naturally. Isaac was the one who told me, "When you're on the streets, you may know stealing is wrong, but it's survival."

A few years ago I was asked to work on a task force to launch a church within the Bellamy Correctional Facility for men in Ionia, Michigan. After several meetings and an agreement with the Michigan Department of Corrections, the church, named Celebration Fellowship, began. The church has the same mission and priorities as many other community churches. A pastor on-site in the prison works with the prison chaplain and prisoners on the liturgies and leads the worship services as people would in other denominations. Many volunteers who are members of churches in the community come in for the Bible studies and to worship with the prisoners. It is also anticipated that prisoners who are released will be more likely to find church homes in the community just as Isaac found a church when he was released. (In fact some of those released have found jobs and supportive churches affiliated with the prison ministry.)

I saw the new church as an excellent opportunity for the prison and volunteers. Prisons benefit from having well-trained volunteers provide services that Corrections' employees either can't or don't have time to offer. Another benefit of the church for prisoners is that they take responsibility for worship services, and by becoming a church community with volunteers, influence the prison environment in a positive way.

In addition the results of faith-based research are favorable. As recently as August 2010, *Corrections Today* cited a 2002 meta-analysis by the University of Pennsylvania of forty-six studies of religious programs that indicated "higher levels of religious involvement are associated with lower rates of delinquency among youth and reduced criminal activity among adults." Even a critic of faith-based programs concedes that religious programs "run by deeply caring people" may change lives.[3] Given the needs of ex-offenders for services and mentors, religious volunteers have also helped ex-offenders in the community.

3. Cei, "Faith-Based Programs Are Low-Cost Ways to Reduce Recidivism," 49.

I anticipated that the volunteers from the community, when they worshipped with the prisoners, would become familiar with prisoners who wanted to change their lives. When volunteers visit, prisoners see someone from the community who cares enough about them to volunteer. The volunteers are doctors, attorneys, business people, teachers, and pastors. Many work during the day and come in at night. Some are retired. Worship with the prisoners provides them opportunities to connect with prisoners in powerful and meaningful ways. I saw the church in the walls as a "win-win" for volunteers, prisoners, and the prison employees.

After working in the prisons, I did not want to return to prison as a volunteer myself, waiting to go through three gates, and waiting to be searched, and waiting and waiting for the prison meal to be over for the services to begin. I planned to go to one service when everything was in place.

But I did not wait long the first evening I attended a service. The services are held in a school. I was searched as all the volunteers were and walked with an officer escort to the classroom where the prisoners were standing, all in uniform as though they were waiting for a drill sergeant to give them a command to salute. Instead they were singing the hymn, "I've Decided to Follow Jesus, No Turning Back, No Turning Back." I couldn't turn back either. After participating in the Bible study and worshipping with the men, I knew I would be back, even though I'm not always comfortable there.

During my career I talked with many prisoners about various issues and policies related to their incarceration in one way or another. I heard complaints and comments about their personal property, the way an employee or other prisoners behaved, the need for more recreation and programs, the visiting rules, and many other issues. Their comments began with the formal, "Deputy," or "Deputy Libolt." The volunteers wear name tags with their first names. I tried to flip my tag over to be incognito. I didn't want them to recognize me. I found it intrusive the first evening I worshipped when one of the prisoners addressed me using my first name, "Adria," and for another one during a Bible study to ask, "Adria, what do you think about this verse?"

The prisoners are often intense. They have been stripped of freedom and the possessions to which we have become accustomed. They live with anxiety in an often crowded environment with many others they can't trust. Under those foxhole conditions, God has immediacy for them. Lennie Spitale in *Prison Ministry* asks, "Where else can you find so many who know they have done wrong and, in most cases, readily admit it? Where else can you find so many who are genuinely sorry for what they have done? Where else can you find so many broken, hurting, lonely people all collected together in one small space?" [4] For them, the Bible is not abstract. They don't necessarily take it literally, but they take it seriously. It is the Word of Hebrews 4:12, "living and active. Sharper than any double-edged sword, it penetrates even to dividing soul and spirit, joints and marrow; it judges the thoughts and attitudes of the heart." The prisoners at Celebration Fellowship wouldn't understand anemic, watery religions that swing in different directions of one's choosing or whatever is popular at the moment. They might be puzzled by claims of being "spiritual" but not religious.

They grapple with the often harsh conditions of prison day to day and seek real solutions to their problems. While I am inclined to say, "Not so fast" when talking about my faith, they expect God to be on the agenda. They get to the point. Those of us worshipping sense the Holy Spirit moving through the service. When they sing the words of old hymns such as, "Nearer My God to You," and "I Need You Every Hour," their prayers and pleading seem to come from a deep place, from hearts that are longing for God.

I had a lump in my throat when I walked in and heard the brothers sing, "No Turning Back, No Turning Back." I want to believe that none of them will turn back to a life without God once they say their lives have changed. I am skeptical of prisoners' long-term commitments to religion once they are released to the community. I want to see measurable evidence of positive change. In fact, the brothers who have been released have low recidivism rates. Perhaps they won't turn from their faith, but are they supporting their families, establishing positive relationships, as well as living law-abiding lives? Maybe they will find supportive people and churches, but I know some of them like Isaac may commit another crime, and return to prison. If they do, many of us will not be able to turn our backs on them. We have seen Isaac and the faces of the Celebration Fellowship Church in the prison.

---

4. Spitale, *Prison Ministry*, 190.

23

Godsons and Godsends

He wasn't looking for lists, but [for] someone to listen.

—ADRIA LIBOLT

MY HUSBAND AND I have a godson. "Brad" was not even in elementary school when we spent a cold day cross-country skiing and sledding with his parents and him. Perhaps his parents had hopes of us establishing a relationship with him after we signed the guardianship papers. Every time I opened the file drawer where his papers were, I saw the file with his name, but the significance of the papers is not something we thought about very much. Brad's parents were young and healthy, and he was an only child. We wanted children, but he would have plenty of attention. As he was growing up, we didn't have more of a relationship with him than with some other children in our church. I've asked myself why we didn't see him more or reach out to him. Perhaps we were distracted with work and all of our activities. It wasn't intentional, but we didn't give him much thought.

His parents drifted away from our church and Brad boarded at a good high school in Detroit. When he graduated from high school he came back to church to take classes to make his profession of faith. We began to know him as the exceptional young man he had become—no thanks to us. He has made his parents proud. He is courteous, handsome and well-spoken. He plays hockey and is a good student. We have been able to support him a little as he goes on to college where he is pursuing a pre-med degree. He chose the college he will be attending because it has a reputation for its students studying hard. We are delighted he has come into our lives again, though he took more initiative for that than we did.

By all indications, our godson will do well. Oh, he may struggle financially with college since the one he's chosen is expensive. But if past success is an indication of his future, he will continue achieving. He has supportive parents, a good education, and many advantages.

Not long ago another older but still young man, Jaime, contacted me. I met him several years ago when I was deputy warden in a prison where all the young men twenty-one and younger sentenced to prison came. I had heard he would be coming to the prison where I worked because I knew Jaime through his family in the church. His father had been a volunteer in prison ministry. When Jaime was discharged from prison a few years ago, he reentered the community.

Like our godson, he was courteous, charming and handsome. Like our godson, he had tremendous potential. In another way, the two young men demonstrate the dramatic contrasts in our society between the young people who go beyond parents' expectations and those living on the margins—those who are poor, disadvantaged, unemployed, uneducated, and coming from blended and broken homes.

Jaime was not only an ex-offender but a sex offender trying to live in a society that is intolerant of such offenses. While some offenders have been convicted of rape and child molestation, many of the young men I interviewed in the prison had sex with underage girls. All sex offenses are serious, but sex offenders are often lumped together as though they've all committed the same crime. Restrictions on where they may live when released from prison are rigid. Regardless of what they've done, some of them may not live within a certain distance of where children live or attend school.

National Public Radio has reported that sex offenders have resorted to living under overpasses because they are prohibited from living in many neighborhoods. Despite the criticisms and actual failings of the church, a pastor named Dick Witherow is trying to help this population dumped off under bridges.[1] Overwhelmed with all the problems in society, people have little tolerance for this segment. Sex offenders are the new untouchables like "lepers," a term Pastor Witherow also uses. I was determined to help Jaime.

---

1. Witherow, "Sex Offenders Forced to Live Under Miami Bridge," no pages.

Jaime was trying to live in Grand Rapids where his stepmother and some of his family lived. He contacted me by telephone at the beginning of the summer, and we had talks, sometimes once a week. Although he had asked me to come to Grand Rapids to see him, I had trouble finding time during that summer. "We need to get together," we'd say, but he had that smile in his voice, and I thought he was doing okay. The most he asked of me was a hygiene kit. I began contacting several people who put me in touch with agencies who could give him those kits and other necessities in the city where he lived. He was borrowing a cell phone from a friend so he had it mornings and afternoons until 3pm to talk with me, but it was hard to have long conversations on the phone.

One day he sounded depressed and almost desperate, and told me he might become homeless. He said, "I can't go back to prison again. I just can't." He had not talked like that before. He was usually in good spirits, almost always smiling, but I realized he was asking for more than a hygiene kit.

I asked questions, reminded him of his strengths, anything so he wouldn't be so discouraged, and told him to contact some community groups and agencies I'd recommended. I assured him they could easily provide some help. Shortly after that conversation he asked me to drive to where he lived so we could talk. I had some vacation and was nearly finished painting my garage so I made arrangements to see him.

We have a team at our church helping ex-offenders, and although Jaime had not contacted us, Ralph, one of the people who started the team, wanted to come with me to talk with Jaime. I welcomed the assistance. Our team had identified several principles. Males should work with male ex-offenders. The dynamics of males and females in private relationships working together may be fraught with distractions and attractions. In addition, teams as models of the way community works provide accountability. Another advantage is the additional knowledge and access to community resources teams have compared to any one individual. Another advantage became apparent. Someone other than me may have been able to detect what troubled Jaime and responded to him in a way that was more helpful.

Ralph, who was willing to go with me to talk with Jaime, had a meeting the day I scheduled with him. It didn't matter. Jaime was like family, and I went alone. On a Thursday, August 6, 2009, I finally met him at a restaurant for breakfast.

He drove up in a car with a young lady. I met Annie, and she drove off to work while Jaime and I had breakfast. We talked about many things. "I want to be honest," he said. Annie had been the "victim" in his last crime. She was underage at the time, and her mother had reported him. Now he was seeing her again, and her parents knew.

Many offenders, after release from prison, form relationships with their victims who have come of age. He also talked about the woman, a relative, whose phone he used from 7am to 3pm. He was likable and attracted women.

I tried to get him to talk about work and jobs. Jaime had good personal skills and opportunities, but I sensed he had not pursued work with much passion. In fact, I thought he didn't have his mind on work. He was checking his cell phone, but I doubted his calls were related to work. I asked him what he really wanted to do, and he told me he'd wanted to go to cosmetology school, and knew someone who might be able to get him in.

I came armed with organizations where he could go. I wanted to take him to at least one of the agencies available in Grand Rapids offering services to ex-offenders. I drove him to the Criminal Justice Chaplaincy (CJC) Office on Fulton Street where we met the Director, Jim, who gave him all kinds of suggestions about people to contact. He also gave Jaime a clothing voucher and hygiene kit. He tried to steer him to a training program, and told him how to register for jobs. He'd be provided a mentor. Jaime had no excuses for refusing all the help offered. I was encouraged and optimistic. But when the Director left the room for a few minutes, Jaime said to me, "But you're my mentor."

I said, "No, I can't be. I'm not living here. I'm also leaving on a vacation for a few weeks." I didn't say that a male mentor would be best for him.

As we were walking out the door, I asked him to keep a journal of his activities related to finding a job and place to live, and his thoughts and feelings. I hoped he'd reflect on his life, and see the patterns of drifting I saw. We'd talk again when I returned from vacation.

He was polite, always smiling but he had a faraway look. Was he overwhelmed? Did he ever intend to take advantage of the help offered? What did he expect from me? Was he disappointed about what I'd told him?

We walked to the parking lot, and I drove to an apartment complex where I dropped him off. One of the last things he said to me was, "You know my sister was my age when she was killed." I did know. His sister was brutally murdered, and the case has not been solved. The murder must have weighed on his mind. I left him, satisfied he had help, and that I'd referred him to all the right people. Those other people.

I left messages when I tried to call him from vacation. I never talked with him again. A month after I met with him he was found in a car, dead, the gun beside him. I ask: Where did he get a gun? He wasn't violent. The police reported no footprints led to that car, but his father doesn't believe it. Was he protecting himself from someone? Could I have done anything to prevent his death? What was so important in my life that I didn't go see him earlier when he first called me? Would it have made a difference? Like a dog with a bone, I gnaw at the questions. I grieved with this father. Jaime is his Absalom (2 Samuel 18).

Perhaps Jaime was far too depressed to take advantage of any solutions. I saw the Jaime I wanted to see and thought I could help, but I know he had a life I didn't see, either the one he was connected to by cell phone, or his own internal and dark world.

At times I have felt strong tugs to help people. A calling may begin as a signature on some guardianship papers, making a commitment to be a parent to someone else's child, like Brad, in the event something happens to them, or it may begin with a request to be a part of someone's life, like Jaime. Looking back, I see I delayed going to see him because I thought we had time, and that maybe I was one of the last people in a long line of people he contacted who could not help him.

Although I know many prisoners leave prison with the same problems they faced going in, Jaime seemed better prepared to adjust than other ex-offenders, so I thought. But discerning what others need is difficult. It requires a close walk with them and others. I knew of resources to offer him, but I wasn't with him often enough to know what his other needs were. Being homeless was the worry he mentioned, but perhaps shelter was second to being estranged from community. He may have been surrounded by people and lonely.

Agencies helping ex-offenders navigate their way back to the world are necessary, but they do not take the place of caring about someone. Jaime was not a project or possession, or a statistic of failure or success, but a person desperately in need of love and perhaps some medication.

People who want to end their lives often do, but did Jaime want that, or was there something or someone else who could have helped? Answers were easier before he left. All I can do now is ask whatever "Jaime" crosses my path how I may help him, and make sure that I do.

24

Larry, Hard Hearts, and Unspoken Words

Preach the Gospel always: use words when necessary.

—FRANCIS OF ASSISI

LIKE MOTHS TO A flame, many men and women who are incarcerated are drawn to God. They have reached a point when even those who love them the most cannot release them from their "chains." In these circumstances many who know how futile it is to rely on others turn to God for the first time.

In December 2007, Chandra Bozelko, a Princeton graduate with post-graduate study under her belt, was convicted of identity theft and illegal use of a credit card, and sent to York Correctional Institution in Niantic. In an article called "The God of Ambition," in *Commonweal*, January 28, 2011, she writes about the piety and phony religious expressions around her, and reasons, "God is not supposed to be a last resort."[1] Like Marx's claim that religion is the opiate of the masses, she compares prisons to foxholes without atheists, and refers to prisoners finding religion as a "cliché." When I read Chandra's words, I thought about Larry.

A committee of our church with members from other churches is committed to helping prisoners and ex-offenders, like Larry, make the transition from prison to the community in modest ways that we are still learning. Some of us worship with prisoners at Celebration Fellowship in the Bellamy prison in Ionia, Michigan, where prisoners expect to hear about God. Larry is an ex-offender who does not want us to talk to him about God.

1. Bozelko, "The God of Ambition: From Princeton to Faith," 18.

Larry's adoptive father came to us before Larry was released from prison and asked us to help him. We had several meetings before he was paroled, and several members of the committee picked him up on the day of his release.

More than one person had called Larry "hard-headed" and "arrogant." He's bright, artistic, and courteous, but had not always made himself attractive to those of us who were committed to helping ex-offenders. He had social skills, but often a sad look weighed down his handsome face, and we hoped the mental health counseling he received would help him keep his spirits up.

Larry did not ask many questions of us, or seem very interested in anyone on the team, though he expressed his gratefulness to men on the committee who gave him rides to various agencies before he had a car. That chip on his shoulder and blaming others for his problems were other concerns we had. Larry's comments about the Michigan Department of Corrections (MDOC) were often derogatory and showed his limited view of what Corrections does. He did not talk about his weaknesses or show remorse about what led to his incarceration, but it is also true that we tend to encourage ex-offenders to look ahead and focus on their futures in the community instead of dwelling on their time in prison.

When he was paroled, Larry found a job where he had previously worked in hotel management, an area in which he was skilled. He began complaining about the hostile atmosphere of his workplace. What sometimes happens in prison, and what happened at his worksite, was that he got himself noticed. Supervisors warned him, and then he told others to "watch out for problems, you'll be next." Although he did not mean it in a threatening way, employees and supervisors interpreted his actions that way and soon let him go.

We encouraged him to pursue other jobs. People from the church wrote letters on his behalf for other employment opportunities. Other church members offered him part-time temporary jobs in landscaping. His need for work was announced in the church bulletin. He attended workshops on writing resumes at the church.

When he had a parole hearing, several of us went with him to encourage him and be supportive. The meeting was positive. He was meeting his conditions for parole and doing what was asked of him, including attending the counseling sessions, and continuing to search for employment, or so he told us.

We have been reluctant to give ex-offenders financial help. But when Larry couldn't pay his bills, he came to us with a request for financial assistance. Another church committee approved the loan. He is proud, and I knew how hard it must have been for him to ask.

I don't know anyone, with the exception of his adoptive father and the woman who provided him housing, who has helped him more than people in the church. When we see him, we often take him out for breakfast or a meal. Even though Larry didn't find God in prison like many do, he may see the love of God in the people who work on his behalf, though he made it clear he doesn't have much use for religion.

Recently, I saw a letter to the editor of a newspaper with remarks about the Bible, signed by Larry. "It is religious historical fiction, filled with presumptions, misconceptions and wishful thinking," he wrote. Larry made his position clear to us from the beginning. He did not share our beliefs. We didn't expect him to go to church or become a Christian just because we were helping him.

Our committee does not help ex-offenders expecting something in return, though we like to see them get jobs and become more independent. The letter to the editor was not a personal slap in the committee's face, though I didn't expect a public repudiation of the Bible either. One of the committee members said with a smile, "He may not be very far along in his faith journey."

Perhaps he expects our help because of what we believe, and we are being taken as do-gooders or people who should be helping ex-offenders like him. He may not realize that what motivates us is the book he thinks is "filled with presumptions, misconceptions and wishful thinking." The Bible is clear about helping the poor, the imprisoned, and others on the margins, regardless of whether or not we like them. It doesn't say certain beliefs or preaching are required.

Some ex-offenders have charming personalities. They are people to whom we're naturally attracted. They are grateful and may spend more of their time writing thank you notes than writing critical comments about religion or the Bible. They are easier to help than those like Larry.

We work with the people who come before us with their faults and imperfections not because they are the easiest people, but simply because they have needs, and we are called to respond to them.

Larry has continued to see and meet with us for over a year, and we know him better each time we meet with him. We hear he works hard at his odd jobs. He has a wry sense of humor and seems honest. He is not manipulative, and his steadiness has shown us what to expect of him. Several people on the committee continue giving him rides and contact him regularly to see how he's doing. When I e-mail him, he responds and is articulate. He is beginning to mentor other ex-offenders who are released.

Larry has brought us together. We are a committee with tasks becoming a community with a new perspective and insights about what it means to reach out to someone who may be using us while rejecting the church. I remind myself that even though we are realistic about Larry's dependence and requests, our help and care is not conditional. If we assumed everyone we assisted saw God at work, we would be mistaken. To see Larry as another man to win over to Christianity is dehumanizing. We are not gods who have the answers but believers with weaknesses and needs, and ex-offenders like Larry are more than recipients of resources. Still, words about our faith as well as actions may make us more present to Larry. Tiptoeing around language about God seems artificial and insincere.

Several years ago, I went to a hotel for a retreat with pastors and other church representatives. Our speaker, a man named Peter, who taught classes at a seminary, told us that many students have less trouble arguing and reasoning than talking about what God has done and is doing in their lives. In fact, he claimed, talk of God is all around us, and Christians often don't hear it.

In my experience faith is a personal matter. We did not tell stories of God's grace in our individual lives. When I was growing up, adults had plenty to say about their beliefs, but it tended to be analytical with discussions related to theology and doctrine. Peter told us he gives his students a short structure to present Christ to others quickly and easily because sometimes all we have is five minutes. Few people have the patience to listen to long theological discourse.

During our break, I went to the restroom where I met an attractive young lady on her way out. Her dark brown hair was shiny, and she wore a stylish blouse with ruffles. Our eyes met in the mirror, and she smiled. She washed her hands while I checked on my hair and lipstick. "We are in the room next to yours. What are you doing here?" she asked.

I told her about our group of pastors and church representatives, and gave her some general information about the retreat.

"Sounds like fun," she said.

"What are you doing here?" I asked.

"Drinking," she said. "We're in the bar. I've taken the Dale Carnegie course, and it changed my life," she said, and just that quickly she was walking away while it was dawning on me to say, but, but, wait! What changed my life was Jesus. I imagined her going back to her group in the bar and telling them she saw someone in the restroom and told them about how Dale Carnegie had changed her life.

I have a history of hoarding Jesus. Jesus saves, but I've saved Jesus. I wait for just the right time to talk about Jesus, and it slips away, like looking for just the right time to get a pet or have a baby, and it never comes.

When I worked in the prisons, employees knew my husband was a pastor. They wore What-Would-Jesus-Do (WWJD) bracelets, and at one prison they bought me a necklace with a cross for a good-bye gift. How many opportunities did I have, and miss, to talk with them about personal matters of faith because I thought I could not do so in a state institution or was afraid I'd offend someone?

Chandra Bozelko, the Princeton graduate who went to the York Correctional Institution, eventually found God in prison. He came with the help of Deacon Dolan, an educated and brilliant preacher, and a person she respected. He explained theology in a way that reached the prisoners.

Larry walked away from prison walls and for now, stays outside the church's walls, except for our meetings. Perhaps he is waiting to hear the right words from the right person. Perhaps like Jesus' parable of the sower scattering seed, some has been trampled, choked among thorns, eaten by birds, or suffocated without moisture on the rocks, and Larry is waiting for the right conditions to receive the Word. Maybe, because of him, we are the ones on the path being transformed so we can flourish in our work with ex-offenders.

25

Monica, Forgiveness, and Heart Work

*"True forgiveness deals with the past,
all of the past, to make the future possible."*

—ARCHBISHOP DESMOND TUTU,
NO FUTURE WITHOUT FORGIVENESS

"I MISS YOU MY friend and don't you forget that."

Monica's messages by e-mail often end with a closing like that. During the last year she has written to me every few days though I would prefer seeing her more often.

Our prison ministry and reentry church committee helps one ex-offender—Larry, described in chapter 24—in whatever ways we can because it is right, even though his personality doesn't endear him to us. Our help to him is not always a matter of the heart.

My reaction to Monica is the opposite. She has a good heart, and draws people to her. I not only want to help her in any way I can, I like being with her. Her energy and passion are contagious. Sometimes, a small voice or distrustful intuition tells me to be careful. Her past crime is serious. I rationalize trusting her.

The author Jane Jacobs writes that without basic mutual trust, little commerce and business activities can occur in our society. A Presbyterian minister Dr. Frank Crane says, "You may be deceived if you trust too much, but you will live in torment if you don't trust enough." But I read many prisoner files, and know likeable offenders can fool us. I wonder if she distrusts me, or if there's another reason she stays away.

I first heard about Monica at a church meeting where a few of us were making arrangements to pick up another ex-offender from a prison. Her name came up because she worked at ARRO, (Advocacy, Reentry, Reintegration and Outreach) a non-profit agency that helps people released from prison. "Monica?" I asked.

Bob was glad to talk about her. "She does a great job helping out other ex-offenders."

"What's her last name?" "Monica" is a common name, and the chances I'd know her were slim. Several people, including an intern from my church working at ARRO, told me what a good job she was doing.

As I've mentioned, during my career in Corrections I worked at several prisons and at one of the only two women's facilities. I did not work at the women's facility long, but the female prisoners left an impression. I remembered Monica vividly. I could see her standing in her cubicle as I made my rounds and recalled talking with her. She had a good sense of humor and was assertive without being surly or defensive. She never seemed to have hidden agendas, and conversing with her was easy.

I wanted to see her but wondered if she would remember me or would have any interest in seeing me. Perhaps she would not want to hear from anyone associated with prison, especially employees who had been authority figures. I imagined prisoners released into the community might avoid those prickly people who enforced the rules and reminded prisoners of what they could not do. I hesitated calling her. Several weeks later I received an e-mail from her.

> Bob gave me your e-mail address, and said you'd like to see me. I can't tell you how excited I was to hear that you might even remember me, God works his ways for sure. I am working at ARRO, a grassroots reentry program, and I was voted on the Ingham County Board of Commissioners, Corrections Advisory Board and try to offer my experience and do all I can do to help others, just like when I was in prison.
>
> I wanted to tell you how excited I was to even be able to attempt to make contact with you. I hope you will respond.

When I responded to her e-mail, I indicated my surprise about her involvement. A parolee working on boards and with other agencies while she helps other ex-offenders? In this economy? What was she like after so many years? I was resisting my stereotypical perceptions of ex-offenders, but was there a typical ex-offender? She could be doing exceptionally well. After answering her e-mail, I received another one.

Ms. Libolt

I can't tell you how excited I was to get your response. I don't let my past get in my way, I made a mistake and I learned from it, and my mission in life is to help others. I have been working with MDOC with ARRO, and I even spoke to a warden the other day. While I know that you were my keepers, you are all people and there to do a job, and even if I didn't seem to respect authority, I honestly did. I just had my own anger issues at my own injustice and I seemed to use the MDOC to lash out in my own pain.

One thing I really want to do is to help change the public perception about ex-felons. It is so hard on me at times to have people look down on me. I know I committed a crime, but I did 28 years too and helped so many while I was there. If God can forgive me, then people should stop trying so hard to put road blocks in the way.

Our program has just lost so much grant money that they cut my hours to fifteen so I have been out trying to find more work. I would love to do my own re-entry program for those that did lots of time like myself. It is so amazing to me that you are trying to help females that have been incarcerated, you are awesome.

I would love to meet for coffee or something. Just have to tell you I still have left over issues about eating in public, I haven't gotten over that 20 minutes to swallow the food, but since you understand where I have been I won't have a problem.

Hope to hear from you soon.

Thank you so much,
Monica

We e-mailed each other regularly.

I am humbled by her desire to change public perceptions about ex-felons and feel sorry if people are looking down on her. *"If God can forgive me, then people should stop trying so hard to put road blocks in the way."* Yes, some crimes are so abhorrent we can't seem to get beyond them to accept a person. Forgiveness is the last thing on our minds.

Her compliments move and embarrass me. I ask her to call me by my first name—no titles. I want her to treat me as a friend and not a supervisor. I tell her I enjoy our mutual friendship and don't feel obligated to be with her because she is an ex-offender. After several attempts to get together, we finally meet.

She orders corned beef sandwiches, and I walk in the ARRO office to have lunch with her. I choke up. She looks the same though I do not remember her being so thin. Her dark blonde hair is shoulder length and she is dressed professionally, wearing high heels. We embrace, and she introduces me to several people in her office, some of whom had been in prison. She tells me she had cancer about the time she went on parole and completed a regimen of chemotherapy treatment.

The ARRO office is full of activity, but Monica cannot stay in her chair so her movements make the agency look busy. She is answering her cell phone or getting up to help someone, and she does not finish her sandwich and gives half of it to someone. The woman says, "I was wondering what I was going to do for lunch"—by which I do not think she was trying to decide which restaurant she would be going to that day. As Monica says in her e-mail, eating in the prison is not a leisurely dining experience, and eating in front of people is not comfortable yet. She doesn't finish her lunches, but she is as generous with food as she is with time for others.

Monica talks about several women who served time with her in prison as though they are her family. I remember some of them. In addition to the people she works with at ARRO, they are her community still.

She tells me about her work with the people who come in for services, people like Quincy and Boston who come in and complain. Boston talks about how difficult it is on the streets, and about getting on disability, maybe getting some money from the state. Monica says, "C'mon Boston, why are you going to ask for support from the state? You're done with all that. Get a job." But she doesn't mind when they come in. She knows it's a connection—to the past and maybe the future, and how to relate to them.

Quincy gets a job for the Salvation Army ringing the bell. He is excited. "Maybe I'll call Mom, tell her I have a job."

Monica tells me reality sets in quickly. You sit on your bunk in prison and dream of what you'll do. Ex-offenders hit the streets, and they must make all the decisions made for them in prison. Boredom sets in too, and soon they are living their same lives, only outside the walls. I think of the Peggy Lee song, "Is That All There Is?"

Monica tells me when she was in prison she worried the whole time her mother would die before she got out, and now she wants to take care of her. Her mom is very supportive and proud of her. Perhaps Monica inherited her good heart from her mother. Her parole agent tells Monica she watches out for everyone, but must care for herself.

She likes talking about her accomplishments in prison—how she graduated and earned her college degree. When she tells me some employees in the prison behaved as though she didn't deserve a degree, her eyes flash with irritation. She tells them, "Look, I was working on this degree before I went to prison, and I'm finishing it."

She knows children suffer when their mothers go to prison, and she helped start a program for children of incarcerated women. ARRO works with some of those children. Her advocacy work continues here at ARRO and entails fighting to "ban the box," the little box that alerts employers the applicant committed a felony. She works on ensuring ex-prisoners have IDs and driver's licenses.

When I see what she is doing for others, I think perhaps the best way to help her is to walk beside her, volunteer at ARRO and help her do what she loves doing. But she may want to help and not be helped. Didn't we hope against the odds that returning citizens would be independent? She e-mails almost daily thanking me for being a friend and indicating how important it is to her.

"I miss you my friend and am so lucky to have you in my life. Monica."

I respond to her e-mail, and ask when I can see her, but she has a meeting or has decided to go out of town for the weekend. I thought I made friends easily, but we have not seen each other much.

She is working part-time but tells me she is very busy. I hear this from others released from prison, too. The sudden fast pace of their world is exhausting, and a type of post-release stress is often the result. Monica tells me it is harder getting out than going into prison. She says she has poor time management skills. Maybe. And maybe I make her nervous. She is hyperactive, getting up from the table, not finishing lunch—distracted. Parole status consumes energy. A woman in a prominent position in the community who lost a family member in a violent crime and is on a board with Monica asks, "Why is a former prisoner on this committee? Who does she think she is?"

> "You do not make me feel uncomfortable. You have helped me so much with my many issues and make me feel accepted and I can't tell you what that means to me."

But people have not trusted her, and she may not trust me and can't tell me. I cannot take back my position as an authority figure in her life even though I worked only a short time at the women's prison. Maybe she's afraid of being with me because she's afraid I'll find out too much about her. For all her energy and all her talk about her new apartment and her puppy, I feel there is something she is not telling.

Perhaps I know her better than I would if we were not e-mailing. While we communicate regularly, the nature of paper and pen or e-mail writing is separation. We are not communicating with the immediacy of the physical that face-to-face communication provides, and I don't hear her intonations or the feelings in her words as I would if we talked on the telephone. I ask lots of questions and then apologize for asking them, and she responds, *"You never wear me out with your questions, please always ask."* But she doesn't always answer those questions. We don't always look at the e-mails of a few days ago as we move to other days and priorities.

Then I received this message, after I stopped at the funeral home when her brother passed away: "Please say some prayers for me as I am not doing good at all. But you're on my mind and I cherish our friendship." In another e-mail, "Please know that your friendship and support means the world to me and I will call as soon as the phone lets me. I am so blessed to have so much love in my life." But we haven't seen each other since the memorial service.

We exchange a series of long e-mails when I try to help her before she goes to a job interview. She knows the people who interview her for the opening at a community agency related to Corrections. They are familiar with "her case" and her work in advocacy. She is conscientious about her preparations for the interview. But the burden of her incarceration weighs her down, and she knows or imagines others underestimating her.

> "Once I am off parole I know that I can do lots more. Some people have tried very hard to look down on me rather than realize the value of my experience and knowledge. I am so tired of people thinking that I can't have good input, instead they ignore me. One person tried to get me taken off the corrections advisory board because I was on parole. But once I don't have to worry about the threat of them sending me back I will do the things that I know will benefit Lansing and ex-felons…I miss you my friend and can't wait to see you again."

Monica calls me on her cell phone to tell me about her talk at a seminar. A woman, another member on the panel, sitting at her table gets up and moves. She may have her reasons, but Monica thinks it is because she is an ex-offender. "She thinks she's better than me. She doesn't think ex-offenders should be involved in this seminar."

In Corrections we offer programs in the hope that prisoners will be rehabilitated and that once released, they will be restored to the community. But too often people want to remember an offender by their offense that occurred long ago. One notorious prisoner, Kathy Boudin, did not let prison keep her from accomplishing good things herself and for others while she was in prison, but she will be remembered for her crime and incarceration. Like Monica she was also recently paroled.

In 2003, Boudin, the daughter of a civil rights attorney and a former Weather Underground member, was released from a New York prison after serving twenty-two years for murder. She was the passenger in the armored vehicle that left two policemen and one security guard dead. Boudin committed a horrible crime.[1]

Several newspaper articles reported the opposition of family members of the victims and policemen. New York Governor George Pataki took advantage of the continuing grief of family members to discourage her parole. If she had murdered a member of my family, I would have a difficult time seeing her released from prison too. I hang on to small grievances, holding them tightly like precious stones that weigh me down and become a part of me that turns rigid and can no longer bend. I do not forgive easily. Boudin may have managed her time to do whatever she could to better herself and others, but I wondered if she regretted the agony she caused. I wanted to know she felt remorse for what she had done.

An article in the September 15, 2003 *The Nation* reports Boudin's accomplishments while she was in prison. She was instrumental in beginning a program for children of incarcerated parents and a parent education program to help mothers in their parent roles. She wrote an adult literacy program which was used at the prison. She advocated for prisoners' health programs for AIDS and worked on a program to help prisoners continue college. The article says, "Without sentimentalizing or minimizing the seriousness of Boudin's crime, we ought to see in this moment an opportunity to recognize her life in prison as a model for

1. Fitzgerald, "60's radical released after 22 years in prison," 4.

others to emulate—including her work in adult education and also her advocacy on behalf of prisoners with AIDS." [2]

Some would say her accomplishments in prison were the least Kathy Boudin could do to repay her debt to society. Many prisoners are too damaged to change, and may never be able to function without harming others in society. But Kathy had changed.

Boudin refused to let her crime or prison define her life, but others will not forget. Not everyone approved of her parole. Politicians, law enforcement, and victims' families opposed her release. Brent Newbury, president of the Rockland County Patrolmen's Benevolent Association described himself as "physically ill" on seeing Kathy Boudin walk out of prison.[3] Most of us are better at revenge than forgiveness. Forgiveness is unexpected.

Occasionally, I read the true story about Marietta Jaeger to remind myself that those *most* wronged often forgive. The offenders they forgive are those who least deserve forgiveness.

Jaeger could nearly taste revenge when her seven year-old daughter Susie was kidnapped on a camping trip in Montana, and later killed. For over a year before she knew who the murderer was, she wished for his death. Then the killer called her at her home in Michigan to taunt her. But something changed Jaeger's heart. When she asked the killer what she could do to help him, he broke down and wept. When Jaeger refused revenge, the case unraveled, and the killer confessed to the police.

Although she didn't know if the young man could ever be restored to the community, she did not want that possibility denied. She knew the futility of a death sentence and how another death would not honor Susie. The prosecutor recommended imprisonment without parole. Jaeger helped begin Murder Victims Families for Reconciliation.[4]

Jaeger's forgiveness of her child's murderer was not expected. Forgiveness is difficult and may never occur for many victims of crimes as serious as the man who murdered Jaeger's daughter. Forgiveness in such extreme circumstances is costly. But Jesus is clear about forgiveness and how it connects us. We will be forgiven if we forgive others, and if we don't, we won't be forgiven either.

2. Editorial, "Kathy Boudin's Time," 5.

3. Fitzgerald, "60's radical released after 22 years in prison," 4.

4. Jaeger, "Not in My Susie's Name," 34–37.

In October, 2006 Charles Carl Roberts killed four Amish girls in Pennsylvania while they were in school. The Amish families invited Robert's widow to the funeral and donated money to her.[5] Some of the Amish families attended Robert's funeral too and hugged his widow. The media reported that many mistakenly felt the Amish must have gotten over the tragedy quickly though there was evidence they suffered greatly. Yet the community that lost the little girls did the unexpected. They showed the world forgiveness.

Marietta Jaeger whose child was killed and the Amish community know something profound that many of us find hard to understand. We are connected in our brokenness and in our need of forgiveness and community. Revenge fuels hatred, while forgiveness creates a mysterious space for a new reality.

I re-read Monica's email. "If God can forgive me, then people should stop trying so hard to put road blocks in the way."

Many offenders make positive changes in the difficult environment of prison. Sadly, we do not always support them once they are out. Perhaps the best we can do is view this with a practical lens. We may never understand or forgive, but we ignore at our peril ex-offenders and their needs, not only for food and shelter, but their desire to live meaningful lives. We are diminished in our communities if we ignore the many prisoners released after they serve their time. If they are not integrated into our communities, they may commit new crimes or return to prison at great public expense.

The people Monica helps at ARRO are different than the people with whom I typically socialize. They are poor. Some were in prison. Others have siblings and spouses in prison. Those who were rich and led successful lives before they committed crimes may not come to places like ARRO where people, like Monica, generous in so many ways, continue to bump up against barriers, no longer confining them, but *defining* them by their past crimes or imprisonment, rather than by who they have become.

If we call ex-offenders returning citizens, we will expect them to embrace all that being a citizen entails including joining organizations, serving on commissions and boards, and other groups that citizens join.

---

5. Associated Press, "Never got a chance," Lansing State Journal.

They will hold meaningful jobs like Monica who has a passion to help people.

I end this book with a challenge to myself, one that may resonate with you: What obstacles do I put up that keep ex-offenders at a distance? Is it the jewelry I wear or the nice neighborhood I live in, or judgmental looks or things I say? Is it paternalism? Arrogance? I want to break down barriers between Monica and me that keep us from connecting. I want my heart to be as generous and open as hers even if she does not choose my friendship.

The allotment of time for meals in prisons does not encourage friendship as Monica's experience attests. Sometimes dinner is a hurried and noisy affair and often called "chow." Yet before meals, some of the prisoners likely say, *"Give us this day our daily bread and forgive us our debts, as we also have forgiven our debtors."* Like Monica, other prisoners and ex-offenders may be uncomfortable eating around others, but they are hungry for forgiveness and acceptance.

Summary and Themes

WHEN PEOPLE LOOK AT my small frame and express surprise that I worked as a prison deputy warden, I realize we make assumptions about prisons. One of these assumptions, often depicted in the media, is that prisons are full of dangerous offenders and brawny employees who break up prison fights. Although there is some truth to those myths and assumptions, in fact prisons have staff and prisoners of all sizes. Besides being a perfectly fine size I am also the right fit for prison work—so right that it was difficult for me to leave—and my more recent work volunteering in prisons and working with ex-offenders shows that I haven't left.

Just as the women prisoners at the York Correctional Institution for women in Connecticut sang, "Couldn't Keep it to Myself," I was compelled to write this book for many reasons. One is that the stories and experiences recorded in it dispel some myths and assumptions that are perpetrated and reiterated by some politicians and media personnel.

Yet stories and experiences don't provide answers or solutions like math problems. Instead, I hope the reader recognizes in them some of the scenes behind the gates and some of the characters and lives of the prison environment and culture not often portrayed in the media. Newspapers and television capitalize on what is dramatic. Film, for the sake of entertainment, offers stereotypes, vilifying some characters and elevating others. Accurate stories and experiences show life to be more complex and nuanced than that.

I hope the stories and experiences I narrate here reveal what occurs over time inside a prison (and outside, with ex-offenders). Wardens and deputy wardens, along with officers and supervisors, are responsible for operations within the prison, feeling the pulse of the prisons where they are working. Yet books and articles about prisons and prison life are often written by professional writers or journalists, students, and criminal justice professors who have not worked for any length of time in prisons, or at all. While it is true that some prisons are carefully controlled while others are not, some more conservative writers paint a terrible picture of people and life in prison, and others, more liberal, write as though there is no need of maximum prisons to house people who commit horrible crimes. I had a vantage point that many writing about prisons do not have. My boots were on the ground.

Since I have evaluated prisons' programs professionally, I know the importance of asking questions and finding answers through responsible research in a field loaded with strong opinions and passionate beliefs. I know how essential it is to make sound economic decisions based on safety and the best data rather than someone's agenda. I have read material by experts who have not breathed the air in a prison or have spent a short time at only one prison, and their lack of knowledge is often apparent. Their writing doesn't resonate with those who have worked there.

Even professional leaders in corrections who are promoted and skip working inside prisons often lose what makes the place tick as they focus on their own advancement. Leaders who should have the most knowledge sometimes isolate themselves from prisoners or skim over the details of the work and make mistakes. Their employees prop them up instead of relying on them. We assume prison leaders at higher levels have superior knowledge of the workings of prisons, and train and encourage those they supervise. But most of us learned extensively from and were supported by the officers and supervisors within prisons who worked for us.

Stories don't have answers, and yet themes emerge in what is written.

One pervasive theme in this book is fear. I was often asked whether I was afraid working in prisons. I ask: Are prisons as fearful as they are often portrayed? Or are other experiences equally frightening? Fear can either immobilize, or call us to vigilance and urge us to provide for the safety of prisoners and employees.

A few years ago a group of us were in the Dominican Republic where my husband Clay was leading a retreat for missionaries. We were crossing a bridge over the Arroyo Hondo (deep stream) on the way to Lapuya, where some 25,000 poor people have settled, living in a canyon, far below where the rich live in lavish gated communities. Bree, the youngest girl in our group, asked one of the missionaries if crossing that rickety bridge was safe. "No," he said, "but when is it ever safe to be a Christian?"

It's one of the questions I asked about prisons. What makes prison environments safe? How many resources should be spent on security, corrections officers, guard towers, and tough emergency equipment? How much of safety is also repairing doors and locks and fixing the plumbing or whatever is rickety? Is security in a prison also housekeeping, and providing access to adequate health care, food, programs and recreation for prisoners? Fyodor Dostoevsky said, "The degree of civilization in a society can be judged by entering its prisons." I thought often about how we could make more humane the prisons where so many people with different criminal backgrounds are crammed together. I didn't always succeed in this, but I tried to raise the bar while tightening the screws.

Years before I worked in Corrections, when I impulsively drove away a car that didn't belong to me, it didn't occur to me that I'd committed a crime—at least not immediately. I thought it was innocent fun. After all, I'd driven that car before and had the key. During my career in Corrections, I saw many prisoners who had committed crimes like mine and crimes more insignificant. And while I met many excellent employees, others crossed the line in the way they treated other employees or prisoners. The assumption in prisons is that employees do what is right while prisoners are on the other side. Is it that easy? Can we even predict who will be committing crimes?

We are all a mixture of messy humanity, possessing both the capacity to do good and to do terrible things. Prisoners, often discussed and regarded as a separate class, are connected to us, distinguished only by the fact they have been convicted to prison. Most of them return to our communities.

We judge appearances, but things are not always as they seem on the surface; we may need to look deeper. Suppose one housing area seems to have more prison fights than any other. Officers may be good at breaking up fights. They respond quickly. But what factors lead to the fights?

How do women working in prisons affect the environment? What do they offer prisons?

Does being tough and strong mean reacting and responding to emergencies or listening, questioning, watching, and preventing critical incidents? Is a woman who repairs radios so employees can effectively communicate with one another as much a hero as those "coming to the rescue" when there's an emergency?

Later in my career this subtitle appeared on every Michigan Department of Corrections memorandum: *"Expecting Excellence Every Day."* I wondered why it became necessary to include it at the top of each of those documents. How are excellence and competence in the Corrections environment defined? Are quiet, less glamorous skills of preventing emergencies as well as reacting to serious incidents, considered excellent?

Many prisoners have victimized others and have been victimized themselves. Being in prison may exacerbate victimization. How do we respond to them? What should we expect when we volunteer and worship with prisoners?

This book is not about the justice of current issues, like the incarceration of large numbers of prisoners and overcrowding, or restorative justice, though I am concerned about these things. For example, how do we help prisoners who have served their time and return to our communities? While we solve large issues, how do we respond to individual ex-offenders asking for help? What about those like Jaime who spiraled downward and gave up on life? I've seen the fear ex-offenders face trying to adjust to a community where there are few support systems or family to care for them as they search for housing or employment and other services. I've heard the bitterness ex-offenders experience because of the stigma of having a record. Those of us trained and experienced to work with prisoners are equipped to help once they are released. Will we continue to identify them by their imprisonment, or help them make a transition to the community?

When I stole a car, I was not charged or sent to an institution for juvenile delinquents because my family and the community where I came from intervened. Justice looked like mercy to me, but would a person who went to prison for the same offense feel she had been treated justly? How do we show mercy while expecting accountability?

I often wonder who I'd be if I had not married Clay. I also don't know who I'd be if I had not worked for the Michigan Department of Corrections. I might have been a teacher or administrator, but I wouldn't be the same person. Prisoners as well as employees gave me powerful insights about themselves and prison work that shaped and changed my life. My intention with these stories is to open windows into the world of prisons.

The stories are based on experiences that won't let go of me. They trouble, haunt, and amuse me. They simmer with questions. I hope they encourage readers to explore and search for answers as I do. I hope readers also see that the rewarding work with employees, prisons, and ex-offenders requires attentiveness but is full of stimulation, satisfaction, adversity, challenges, conflicts, and joy all at the same time. Doing such work has the potential to change lives forever.

Bibliography

Allen, Greg. "Sex Offenders Forced to Live Under Miami Bridge." Miami: National Public Radio, May 20, 2009.

Amnesty International USA, Group 81. "Thousands of Children in U.S.sentenced to Life Without Parole." New York: Amnesty International and Human Rights Watch, 2005.

Associated Press. "Never got a Chance". Georgetown: Lansing State Journal, October 6, 2006.

Auden, W.H. "September 1, 1939." *Poets.org.* 1997. http://www.poets.org/viewmedia. php/prmMID/15545 (accessed November 6, 2011).

Bailey, Amy F. "State audits cite slipshod tracking of prisoners." Lansing State Journal, Lansing: Associated Press in the Lansing State Journal, April 19, 2005.

Barisic, Sonja. "Sniper Trial Highlights Missed Opportunities to End Spree." Associated Press, 03-11-2003.

Beard, Aaron. "D.A. in Duke case keeping low profile." Lansing State Journal, Raleigh, N.C.: Associated Press, 2007.

Beeler, Art. "Reentry: A Matter of Public Safety." *Corrections Today*, June 2009: 19–20.

Bissinger, Buzz. "Duke's Lacrosse Scandal." *Vanity Fair*, July 2006: 70–79.

Blanchette, Kelley, and Kelly N. Taylor. "Reintegration of Female Offenders: Perspectives on 'What Works.'" *Corrections Today*, December 2009: 60–63.

Bozelko, Chandra. "The God of Ambition: From Princeton to Prison to Faith." *Commonweal*, January 28, 2011: 18–19.

Braucht, George S., and Karen Bailey-Smith. "Reentry Surveys: A Reality Check." *Corrections Today*, June, 2006: 88.

Breazzano, DonaLee. "The Federal Bureau of Prisons Shifts Reentry Focus to a Skills-Based Model." *Corrections Today*, December 2009: 50–53.

Buechner, Frederick. *Wishful Thinking: A Theological ABC.* New York: HarperSanFrancisco, 1973.

Buning, Sietze. "Epilogue." In *Style and Class*, by Sietze Buning, 116. Orange City: Middleburg, 1982.

———. "Wilhelmina." In *Style and Class*, by Sietze Buning, 17. Orange City: Middleburg, 1982.

Caruso, Patricia. "Operating a Corrections System in a Depressed Economy: How Michgian Copes." *Corrections Today*, February 2010: 36–39.

Cei, Louis B. "Faith-Based Programs Are Low-Cost Ways to Reduce Recidivism." *Corrections Today*, August, 2010: 48–51.

Conover, Ted. *Newjack.* New York: Random House, Inc, 2000.

Doyle, James. "CSI: Eyewitness Memory." Lecture at Calvin College, Grand Rapids. January 20, 2006.

Editorial. "Kathy Boudin's Time." *The Nation*, September 15, 2003: 4–5.

Engel, Len, John Larivee, and Richard Luedeman. "An Examination of Four States and Their Budget Efforts." *Corrections Today*, December 2009: 42–45.

Fitzgerald, Jim. "60's Radical Released After 22 Years in Prison." Bedford: Associated Press in the Lansing State Journal, September 18, 2003.

Ford, Beverly Helen Kennedy. "Alleged Craiglist Killer Philip Markoff Found Dead in Jail." New York: New York Daily News, 2010.

Garland, David. *The Culture Of Control: Crime And Social Order In Contemporary Society*. Chicago: University of Chicago, 2001.

Gladwell, Malcolm. "The Naked Face." *The New Yorker*, August 05, 2002: 30–49.

Gonzales, Laurence. "Welcome to Gladiator School." *Notre Dame Magazine*, 1988: 34.

Harris, Jean. *Jean Harris*. New York: Kensington Publishing Corp., 1986.

Hesse, Mario L. "A Snapshot of Reentry in Minnesota." *Corrections Today*, 2009: 64–67.

Innes, Christopher A. "The Simple Solution For Reducing Correctional Costs." *Corrections Today*, February, 2010: 32–34.

Isaak, Harvey. "Scandal in Georgia Prisons." *Fortune News, Vol. XXVII, Number 1*, February 1994: 6.

Jaeger, Marietta. "Not in My Susie's Name." In *Frontiers of Justice, Volume 1: The Death Penalty*, by Editor: Claudia Whitman and Julie Zimmerman, 34–37. Brunswick: Biddle Publishing Company, 1997.

Kaiser, David, and Lovisa Stannow. "Prison Rape and the Government." *The New York Review of Books*, March 24, 2011: 26–28.

Karlgaard, Rich. "His Name is Carlos." *Forbes*. April 23, 2007. http://blogs.forbes.com /digitalrules (accessed November 2, 2011).

Kelling, George L., and Catherine M. Coles. "The Promise of Public Order." *Atlantic Unbound* (Atlantic Unbound, The Atlantic Monthly), January, 1997.

Kime, William L. "Filling prisons doesn't reduce the crime rate." Lansing: Lansing State Journal, 2010.

Lamb, Wally. *Couldn't Keep it to Myself*. New York: HarperCollins, 2003.

——. *I'll Fly Away*. New York: HarperCollins, 2007.

Lane, Barbara Parsons. "Puzzle Pieces." In *Couldn't Keep It To Myself*, by Wally Lamb, 229–30. New York: HarperCollins, 2003.

Leifman, Steven. "Judge Steven Leifman Advocates for the Mentally Ill." *Corrections Today*, April, 2009: 76–78.

Libolt, Adria. "The Pastoral Work of an Ex-Offender." In *Frontiers of Justice, Vol 2: Coddling or Common Sense*, by Claudia Whitman, 112–16. Brunswick: Biddle, 1998.

Lucado, Max. *Fearless*. Nashville: Thomas Nelson. 2009.

Maclean, Norman. *Young Men and Fire*. Chicago: The University of Chicago Press, 1992.

Malcolm, Janet. "Iphigenia in Forest Hill." *The New Yorker*, 05 03, 2010: 34–63.

Martin, Deanna. "Ind. prison officials investigate escape as 2 still on the run." Associated Press, Indianapolis: Associated Press in The Lansing State Journal, July 15, 2009.

Meroth, Peter, and Uli Rauss. *Five Years of My Life: An Innocent Man in Guantanamo*. Amnesty International USA, Spring 2008.

Miller, D. W. "Looking Askance at Eyewitness Testimony." *Chronicle of Higher Education*. 02 25, 2000. http://www.psychology.iasstate.edu (accessed 08 11, 2006).

Montaldo, Charles. "Two Killers Escpe Arkansas Prison." Little Rock: Associated Press, June 1, 2009.

Moushey, Bill. "DNA Evidence Excludes Whitley." *Innocence Institute of Point Park University.* March 07, 2006. http://www.pointpark.edu (accessed 05 06, 2007).

NewsOneStaff. "Georgia Prisoners Use Cell Phones to Stage Non-Violent Protest." *NewsOneStaff.* December 14, 2010. http://newsone.com/nation/newsonestaff2 /georgia-inmates-prison-protest-strikecell-phones/ (accessed 11 3, 2011).

Oppat, Susan. "Fence foils escape try at prison." Ann Arbor: Ann Arbor News, 1984.

Paparozzi, Mario. "Much Ado About Nothing: Broken Windows Versus What Works." *Corrections Today*, February, 2003: 30–33.

Parsons, Barbara. "Reawakening Through Nature: A Prison Reflection." In *I'll Fly Away*, by Wally Lamb, 223. New York: HarperCollins, 2007.

Patzer, Maureen. "Fighting Crime with Science." *Greater Lansing Woman*, 03 2007: 46.

Perkinson, Robert. "The Prison Dilemma." *The Nation*, July 6, 2009: 35–36.

Rilke, Rainer Maria. "Der Panther." In *New Poems*, by Ranier Maria Rilke, translation-Edward Snow. New York: North Point, 1907.

Roberts, Robert C. *Spirituality and Human Emotion.* Grand Rapids: Wm B. Eerdmans, 1983.

Runk, David. "Warden says no 'red flag' ahead of escape attempt." Lansing: Associated Press in the Lansing State Journal, 2010.

Singer, Mark. "Escaped." *The New Yorker*, October 9, 2006: 46–57.

Spitale, Lennie. *Prison Ministry: Understanding Prison Culture Inside and Out.* Nashville: Broadman & Holman Publishers, 2002.

Stannow, David Kaiser, and Lovisa. "The Way to Stop Prison Rape." *The New York Review of Books*, 2010: 37–39.

Travis, Jeremy, Anna Crayton, and Debbie A. Mukamal. "A New Era in Inmate Reentry." *Corrections Today*, December 2009: 38–41.

Twain, Mark. "Notebook." In *Notebook*, 1898.

USA, Amnesty International. "Thousands of Children in U.S. sentenced to The Rest of Their Lives: Life without Parole for Child Offenders in the United States." Amnesty International USA, Group 81, November, 2005.

Weir, Frank. "36 Guards Convicted." *Ingham County Legal News*, April 9, 2009: 1, 5.

Whyte, David. "Courage and Conversation." In *Crossing the Unknown Sea*, by David Whyte, 3–8. New York: Riverhead Books, 2001.

———. *Crossing the Unknown Sea.* New York: Riverhead, 2001.

———. "Keats and Conversation." In *Crossing the Unknown Sea*, by David Whyte, 227–37. New York: Riverhead, 2001.

———. "The Awkward Way the Swan Walks." In *Crossing the Unknown Sea*, by David Whyte, 113–38. New York: Riverhead, 2001.

Wilson, James Q., and George L. Kelling. "Broken Windows." *The Atlantic Monthly*, March, 1982: 29–38.

———. "Making Neighborhoods Safe." *The Atlantic Monthly*, February, 1989: 46–52.

Witherow, Dick. "Dick Witherow Ministers to Sex Offenders in Florida." National Public Radio.

Wuornos, Aileen. Wikipedia. http://en.wikipedia.org/wiki/Aileen_Wuornos.

Wyatt, Ken. "Peek Through Time: Reminiscing about Dale Remling's great escape." Jackson: Jackson Citizen Patriot, Updated website February 25, 2011.